Nanny Reilly

Book 1

a novel by

Annette O'Leary-Coggins

iUniverse, Inc.
New York   Bloomington

Nanny Reilly
Book 1

Illustrations by Russell Dauterman, www.russelldauterman.com

Permission foe use given for four lines of Lord of the Dance, written by
Sydney Carter. Copyright 1963 Stainer & Bell Ltd. Administered by Hope
Publishing Company, Carolstream, Illinois. All rights reserved.

Permission for use given for A Child's Bedtime Song, written by Denid E.
Waitley, Ph.D. The Waitley Institute, Ranch Sante Fe, California.

iUniverse books may be ordered through booksellers or by contacting:

iUniverse
1663 Liberty Drive
Bloomington, IN 47403
www.iuniverse.com
1-800-Authors (1-800-288-4677)

ISBN: 978-1-4502-4648-4 (sc)
ISBN: 978-1-4502-4650-7 (dj)
ISBN: 978-1-4502-4649-1 (ebk)

Library of Congress Control Number: 2010910813

Printed in the United States of America

iUniverse rev. date: 7/26/2010

A Child's Bedtime Song

By Denis E. Waitley, Ph.D.

If I had two wishes, I know what they would be.
I'd wish for Roots to cling to, and Wings to set me free.
Roots of inner values, like rings within a tree,
And Wings of independence to seek my destiny.

Roots to hold forever, to keep me safe and strong.
To let me know you love me, when I've done something wrong.
To show me by example, and help me learn to choose.
To take these actions every day, to win instead of loose.

Just be there when I need you, to tell me it's alright
To face my fear of falling when I test my wings in flight.
Don't make my life too easy, it's better if I try
And fail and get back up myself, so I can learn to fly.

If I had two wishes, and two were all I had,
And they could just be granted by my Mom and Dad.
I wouldn't wish for money, or any store bought things.
The greatest gifts I'd ask for, are simply Roots and Wings.

CHAPTER ONE

One evening, while out picking mushrooms, Nanny and her dog Henry Daly came to Magandy's Pond. Henry liked to sniff his way through the reeds around the pond. It was one of his favorite places, especially when the ducks swam close to the bank. Nanny and her older brother would sometimes spend the summer evenings fishing there.

"One day, Henry Daly," said Nanny, "I'm going to find out what's at the bottom of Magandy's Pond. My brother said it has no bottom, and if I fell in there, I would go all the way to Australia. If I wanted to come back home, I would have to find some magic beans and plant them like Jack did to get the beanstalk to grow. Then I could climb the beanstalk all the way back to Ireland."

"Ah, will ya go away outta that. Ya surely don't believe that, do you?" said a voice from nowhere.

"Who said that?" asked Nanny looking around for Andy Magandy, he's the farmer who owned the field she was in. "Who's there? Where are you?"

"Australia is the land down under, but it's surely not under Magandy's Pond," laughed the voice.

"Come out and show yourself," Nanny said in an agitated voice. "Is it a coward you are? If so, be off with ya, and leave me alone!"

"I'm no coward. Sure, I'm one of the bravest men in Ireland, and if you'll open your eyes and look down instead of looking up in the sky you'll see me," replied the unidentified voice.

Nanny looked to the ground. Sitting relaxed on top of a mushroom with his arms folded as though he was expecting Nanny was the smallest

1

man she had ever seen. He stood about ten inches tall, wore black boots with extra large gold buckles, green trousers, a yellow and green-checkered waistcoat, and a green cape with gold trim that hung to his waist. On his head sat a gold crown sparkling with emeralds. He had sullen green eyes, and a red beard about three inches long all around his jaw line.

"Jeepers," said Nanny in astonishment. "Are you a leprechaun?"

"Aye, Lass, you just hit the nail on the head. I'm a leprechaun all right, but I'm no ordinary leprechaun. I am King Brian," said the little man, reaching for the lapels of his waistcoat and sticking his chest out with pride.

Henry Daly stood at Nanny's side and growled at King Brian. He sensed the little man was up to no good and it was his job to protect Nanny. He pushed his snout into Nanny's hand and whined several times.

"I'm King of all the leprechauns in Coolrainy, and you've been stealing the roofs off our houses," said King Brian, his voice taking on a serious tone.

"I didn't know you lived under the mushrooms," said Nanny. "Nobody told me. I can put them all back, and I'll never do it again."

"It's too late for that," King Brian said with a hint of mischief in his voice. "You owe me a favor, or else I'll have to put you under leprechaun's arrest."

"Leprechaun's arrest? What's that?" Nanny asked, starting to wish she'd never come out to play that day.

"Leprechaun's arrest means that all my leprechauns will surround you and your dog, Henry Daly, right here at Magandy's Pond, and no matter how hard you try, you won't be able to break through the circle of leprechauns, until every mushroom you picked all summer grows back and all my people have the roofs back on their houses," King Brian said, folding his arms over his round belly.

Henry Daly heard King Brian mention his name. He barked one time at him and whimpered at Nanny.

"But that will take weeks," Nanny said. "I have to go home tonight to get my supper, and my big brother is taking me to the fair tomorrow."

"Well, unless you promise to do me a favor, you're going to be under leprechaun's arrest from this very moment, and you'll get no mushroom soup for your supper. Nor will you be able to go to any fair." The leprechaun paced around the top of the toadstool looking small but important. "Not tomorrow, or the day after that, or any day in the near future. Not until all those mushrooms have grown back," King Brian said with a glint of achievement in his eyes. He reached behind his head and tipped his crown down slightly on his brow.

King Brian was a crafty old soul. He knew he had left Nanny no way out. He was feeling like cock of the walk and proud of himself for being so clever.

Nanny didn't like what she heard. Henry Daly took a step towards King Brian and growled again. He knew Nanny was bothered by what she heard.

"I'll set my dog after you," said Nanny. "My brother told me that Henry's grandfather won the greyhound derby in record time, and he left the whole pack at the starting gate. He can catch any rabbit around here, and he surely will be able to catch you."

"Catch me? He would have to be able to run faster than the speed of light to catch me," chortled King Brian. "Watch this. Now you see me, now you don't."

King Brian snapped his tiny fingers and disappeared. All Nanny could hear was laughter. Then King Brian snapped again, and appeared on the mushroom cap, fine as you please.

Nanny knew Henry Daly was fast, but he wasn't magical. He was just a good old dog. "What kind of favor do I have to do?" she asked, wishing she too could snap her fingers and disappear, right back home.

"All you have to do is carry a small sack for one mile to Ballineskar, the next village, and back to me here in Coolrainy on Saturday night after everyone has gone to bed. And if you do that, and meet me right by this mushroom, your debt will be paid and I'll grant you one wish."

King Brian's face tightened and turned very serious, his green eyes clouding. He pointed his finger and looked Nanny right in the eye

"But you have to promise me this," the King said, "under no circumstances are you to look inside the sack. If you do, you'll get no wish from me, or any other leprechaun. Not now or ever, and the biggest mushroom you have ever seen will grow out of the top of your head.

You'll never be able to get rid of it, and everyone will tease you until you cry all the time."

Henry nudged Nanny with his nose and whimpered. She knew he was warning her about King Brian.

"I don't like the sound of that," said Nanny. "If Ned Franey sees a mushroom growing out of the top of my head, he'll be calling me names all day, and so will everyone else." Nanny had visions of her archenemy, Ned Franey, gathering a posse of the village children and following her everywhere, calling her all kinds of mushroom names like 'mold head', 'fungus brain', and 'toadstool girl.'

"I'll do it," said Nanny, giving a confident nod. Her auburn curls emphasized her nod. She looked King Brian in the eye and stood tall. Nanny also knew no matter what, she didn't want to be called names of any kind.

"Do you promise me you won't look in the sack?" King Brian asked.

"I promise I won't look into the sack," answered Nanny, picturing a puffy brown and white mushroom growing out of her head and shuddering.

"Good lass, Nanny Reilly," said King Brian. "Meet me here on Saturday at midnight, and don't tell anyone." The King held his finger to his lips, looking sinister for all his smallness.

With that, Nanny and Henry Daly ran off home. Nanny's thoughts were on King Brian's warning. What would happen to her auburn curls if a mushroom grew out of her head? She never thought of her one wish.

CHAPTER TWO

On Saturday morning Nanny took Henry Daly to the village to mail a letter. The village store also acted as a post office and gas station. Henry stayed outside lying in the sun. He liked to lay with his front paws crossed while he observed the activities of the villagers. Nanny went in to mail the letter. Just as Nanny was paying for the stamp, Ned Franey and his mother walked in. Ned stood behind his mother, looked at Nanny, and stuck his fat tongue out. Nanny frowned at him and looked away.

"How are you today, Nanny?" asked Mrs. Donohue, the owner of the establishment. She was placing a tray of freshly made toffee apples on the counter.

"I have a headache," replied Nanny. Nanny was very worried about the task she and Henry had ahead of them at midnight.

"A headache!" Mrs. Donohue said. "What could possibly give a nine-year-old like yourself a headache?"

Nanny looked at Ned's mother, wishing she could tell her the truth. Ned opened his mouth as if he wanted to say something mean to Nanny, but he couldn't because his mother and Mrs. Donohue would hear him. Nanny sighed with relief, she surely didn't need to hear a smart comment come out of Ned Franey's mouth. Nanny had enough going on with her headache.

Nanny knew she couldn't tell anyone about meeting King Brian at Magandy's Pond. If Ned Franey heard, he wouldn't believe her. He'd be laughing at her and chanting, "Liar, liar, your pants is on fire, your tongue is as long as a telephone wire."

"I think it's the change of weather giving me the headache," Nanny answered as she handed the stamped envelope to Mrs. Donohue.

"Would you like a toffee apple for your headache, Nanny?" asked Mrs. Donohue, her round face turning into a smile.

"A toffee apple!" said Nanny. "Yes, please!" Nanny quickly glanced over her right shoulder and saw Ned Franey crinkle up his freckled nose.

"Here you are, Nanny." Mrs. Donohue handed Nanny a homemade toffee apple, "I hope you're feeling better soon."

"Thank you very much, Mrs. Donohue," replied Nanny. Her frown turned into a smile. It was a rare thing to get a free toffee apple from Mrs. Donohue. "I have to go now. My mother wants me to go straight home and no dilly-dallying." Nanny looked at Ned. She smiled and raised her nose in the air. She suddenly forgot all her woes and walked out of the store licking her toffee apple and leaving Ned Franey frowning. His red freckled face blended with his fiery red hair. Nanny thought about sticking her tongue out at him, but she didn't.

That night Nanny went to bed in her jeans, sweater, and sneakers, which felt lumpy and weird, but what could she do? Henry lay stretched out at the end of her bed. His long tail would occasionally wag and hit the bedpost as Nanny spoke softly to him.

"What if we don't wake up in time, Henry Daly?" wondered Nanny. "Will I wake up tomorrow morning with a mushroom growing from my head?" Nanny shuddered thinking about the events that may occur on Sunday morning.

"Jeepers!" she said, if I wear a scarf on my head, the mushroom will be sticking up underneath it. The whole village will see me at Mass. We'll have to pack our belongings and leave Coolrainy!"

Near midnight, everyone was in bed asleep except Nanny. She put a soccer ball and a pillow under the blankets. That way, if her mother looked in on her, she would think Nanny was there. Nanny and Henry were very careful not to make any noise as they crept out the back door.

It was a full moon so Nanny didn't need her dad's flashlight. Henry Daly struck out first and the two made their way to Magandy's Pond to meet King Brian. Nanny and Henry left the back yard through the gate and jumped over a ditch behind the house. They headed off down Katie's lane.

"You go first, Henry Daly," whispered Nanny, "dogs can see in the dark."

Henry trotted through the gate with his ears pricked and his tail straight up in the air. Nanny walked briskly down the moonlit lane and kept to the center. She was afraid something might jump out at her from either side.

About a quarter of a mile down the lane, Nanny climbed over a wooden fence and Henry crawled underneath. An owl hooted from the tall elm tree down the lane. The hair stood up on the back of Nanny's neck and shivers ran down her spine.

"Let's run, Henry Daly," she said. "We'll get there faster." The two ran across the moonlit field all the way to Magandy's Pond. When they got there, King Brian was waiting on the same mushroom that glowed in the moonlight, he was holding a sack. Henry growled at King Brian and stood close to Nanny.

King Brian was beaming from ear to ear when he saw Nanny. He scowled at Henry, and for a minute, Nanny thought there might be a dog-leprechaun tussle. But Henry Daly stuck close to her legs, though he growled softly every few seconds.

"There ya go, Lass," King Brian said. "Take this sack with this rabbit in it to the middle of Katie's Field in Ballineskar. When you get there, you'll see a rabbit's burrow. Open this sack over the entrance of the burrow and let the rabbit run lickety-split into the burrow. Wait there for a minute with the sack still open and another rabbit will run into the sack. Close up the sack as quickly as you can, and bring it back here to me." The King rubbed his hands together and hunched up his shoulders in delight. "You must be back here before dawn breaks," he warned. "If you're not, a mushroom will start appearing on your head."

King Brian reached into his cloak and pulled out a small shillelagh. He waved it at Nanny as though it were a magic wand. "And whatever you do, don't look in the sack."

The rabbit was making brave attempts to jump from the sack. Henry was moving his head sideways with his ears pricked forward staring at the busy sack. He yelped several times.

"This rabbit is not for chasing Henry Daly," said Nanny, "we have to make sure this rabbit stays right where it is until we get to that burrow."

Nanny felt the top of her head to make sure there was no sign of early mushroom sprouts. She threw the sack over her shoulder and took off across the fields with Henry Daly at her side.

CHAPTER THREE

Nanny was relieved that Henry seemed to know where they were going by the way he trotted along with his nose to the ground. He had the same sense of urgency about him that Nanny had. He led the way across the field and down the bog road to Clancy's footbridge. Even though this was familiar territory and Nanny often fished there, she stayed close to Henry. Everything looked different at night. Everything looked spooky and strange. Large leafy limbs of a big oak tree hung over the footbridge and blocked the moonlight. Henry stopped and sniffed the air several times.

"What is it, Henry Daly?" asked Nanny, her teeth beginning to chatter. "Is there something there?" Nanny felt cold and started to tremble. She saw the outline of something large at the other side of the footbridge. Now she wished she had brought her dad's flashlight.

Henry growled and took two steps towards the predator. Then they heard a snort and the large outline took off at the gallop.

Nanny sighed a sigh of relief. "It's only Tom, the plough horse," she said. "We scared him as much as he scared us."

Tom ran about twenty yards, then stopped suddenly, quickly turned, and stood to attention with his nostrils flaring.

"Don't worry, Tom," said Nanny in a soothing voice. "It's only me, Nanny Reilly, and Henry Daly is with me. I'm sorry we woke you and scared you, but you scared us too. We can't stop and talk to you now, we're in a hurry. And shhh," Nanny put her finger to her lips, "don't tell anyone you saw us."

Tom nickered into the night, sounding comforting and friendly. Nanny let out a sigh and continued across the footbridge in a brisk march. Her curls bounced in rhythm to her every step. The rabbit continued to jump around a little. Henry didn't mind the rabbit so much now. He trotted beside Nanny wagging his tail.

"I'll see you tomorrow Tom," Nanny called out. Tom snorted again and continued to stand to attention until Nanny Reilly and Henry were out of sight.

They marched up the ferny trail on Sarah's hill and down into O'Brien's half-acre. Just ahead of them, Nanny could clearly see Ballineskar and Katie Murphy's whitewashed cottage, tucked into the far corner of her field.

"We're almost there Henry Daly," said Nanny. She lengthened her strides and picked up her pace. Henry did the same.

Finally they reached Katie's field. "Find that rabbit's burrow, Henry Daly," said Nanny, pointing across the moonlit grass. "We'll have to be quick. The sun will start rising in a few hours and I don't want a mushroom growing out of my head."

Henry sniffed his way along, his nose combing the grass and his tail in the air as he zigzagged through Katie's Field. Then he stopped, stood perfectly still, and sniffed the air all around him. He stood tall over the burrow wagging his tail and barked once for Nanny's attention.

"Good boy, Henry Daly," said Nanny. "Now all I have to do is let the rabbit into the burrow and wait for another rabbit to run out into the sack." Nanny was feeling more excited than afraid now. She carefully did all she was told to do. She knelt down by the rabbit burrow and opened the drawstring at the neck of the burlap sack. She could smell sweat from the scared rabbit in the cool night air. The sack was barely large enough to cover the mouth of the burrow and Nanny lost her grip. The frightened rabbit almost slipped away, except Henry Daly was hovering over the whole situation and scared the rabbit into the hole. Nanny regained her hold on the sack and held it as best she could over the burrow. Then in an instant, the sack began to bounce around vigorously. The other rabbit had scampered into it and was fighting very hard to get out. Nanny struggled to tie the drawstring. After several attempts she managed to tie up the sack and she quickly threw it over her shoulder, then she and Henry Daly headed back to Magandy's Pond.

The rabbit in the sack was kicking like crazy. Henry whimpered and whined at the overactive sack. If Nanny had allowed it Henry Daly would take that sack and shake it up and down and around and around.

"Stay quiet in there," Nanny said in a loud whisper; concerned she might awaken the farmers sleeping in the cottages nearby. "You're hurting me," she complained, "My back will be full of bruises. The other rabbit was much quieter than you."

"I'm no rabbit," a high-pitched voice yelled from the sack. "And if you don't let me go, I'll turn your ears into rabbit's ears, then you'll have no doubt in your mind what a rabbit looks like."

"I already know what a rabbit looks like," Nanny said, "so stay quiet in there. I'm taking you back to King Brian, king of the leprechauns of all Coolrainy."

"Don't you dare take me to King Brian of Coolrainy. I am Princess Tara, daughter of King Rory, king of all the leprechauns of Ballineskar. If you take me to King Brian, I will turn your ears into rabbit's ears and your nose into a pig's nose."

Nanny couldn't believe her ears. "Now what will I do, Henry Daly?" she said. "If I look in the sack to make sure I have a rabbit in there, a big mushroom will grow on my head, and if I don't look in the sack I'll grow rabbit ears and a pig's nose."

Nanny sat down on a dew-covered rock and started to cry. Henry Daly sat beside her, licking the tears from her face. Sadness filled his big brown eyes.

Princess Tara made comforting comments, she spoke softly like Nanny's grandma. The Princess said, "If you let me out of this sack, I can help you, and I promise I won't turn your ears into rabbit's ears and your nose into a pig's nose."

"But if I look in the sack, a mushroom will grow on my head and all the village children will be laughing at me, especially Ned Franey. He always laughs at me and calls me names."

"Well then," said Princess Tara, "don't look in the sack. You can let me out without looking."

"But if I go back to King Brian with an empty sack, he'll make a mushroom grow out of my head," whined Nanny "Why did you have to run into the sack anyway? Why didn't you just let another rabbit run into your burrow and you stay put?"

"Because that burrow is my house," Princess Tara replied, as she kept pushing the walls of the sack. "When that rabbit came charging in, I got a fright and came charging out. You had the sack open, it's dark in there, and I couldn't see. I didn't realize I was running into a sack. As soon as I realized, it was too late, you had already tied up the sack, and I couldn't get out."

"But why does King Brian want you? Why does he want to take you away from your father, King Rory of Ballineskar?" asked Nanny Reilly.

"Because he wants the crock of gold," Princess Tara said. "King Brian is my uncle, my father's brother, and is banished forever from Ballineskar. That's why he tricked you into coming here. If he steps foot into Ballineskar, he'll turn into a rabbit."

"He'll turn into a rabbit? Is that a curse like a mushroom growing out of the top my head?" Nanny asked.

"Yes it is," answered the Princess, "and he'll stay a rabbit as long as he stays mean."

Nanny wondered whether Ned Franey could be turned into a rabbit.

"Why was he banished forever? And why does he want the crock of gold?" Asked Nanny.

"He was banished forever from Ballineskar because he played too many mean tricks on people. He wants the crock of gold because whoever has the crock of gold shall have all he or she desires, and King Brian wants all of Ballineskar and Coolrainy."

"But what does that have to do with you? Why does he want you?" asked Nanny, sitting up a little straighter and pushing her sneakers in circles on the cool grass.

"He wants me because he knows my father, King Rory, will give him anything he asks for to get me back," replied Princess Tara.

"Can King Brian really make a mushroom grow on top of my head?" asked Nanny in a sad inquisitive voice. Henry sat beside Nanny and put his paw in her lap. He looked up at her, blinked his soft brown eyes several times and whimpered.

"He can," replied Princess Tara, sounding determined. "And I can turn your ears into rabbit's ears, and your nose into a pig's nose, so you better let me out."

"Can you help me? I don't know what I should do," said Nanny. "I would like to let you go, but I'm afraid King Brian will make a mushroom grow out of my head."

"Of course I can help you, just don't look in the sack. Turn away while I climb out of here. Then when I'm out, we'll make a plan to trick King Brian, and maybe then he'll never trick anybody again," said Princess Tara. "I've learned a trick or two myself." The little Princess punched the side of the sack to punctuate her words.

"OK," said Nanny, "here goes." Keeping her eyes shut, Nanny opened the sack with one hand. She placed her other hand on top of her head. She thought if a mushroom started to grow, she could push it back down.

"Free at last," sighed Princess Tara; sounding much clearer now that she was out of the sack.

"May I open my eyes now?" asked Nanny Reilly.

"You may," answered Princess Tara.

Nanny opened her eyes. Before her, on the grass, stood a girl no more than eight inches tall with long wavy red hair. She wore pink pajamas with tiny green shamrocks all over them, and a gold crown with diamonds all around it on her head.

"You surely are tiny," said Nanny. "You're smaller than King Brian."

"Of course I am," replied the Princess as she wiped her forehead with a tiny pink lace handkerchief. "I still have a lot of growing to do. My mother told me I'm going to grow as tall as my Aunt Betsy, and she's nine and a half inches tall."

The little Princess sneezed. "It was very stuffy in there. Have you ever been tied up in a sack before?" she asked

"No, I haven't," Nanny said, "but Ned Franey locked me in the coal shed once. He told me Henry Daly was trapped in there and couldn't get out. I ran in to rescue Henry Daly, and sure, he wasn't in there at all. Then Ned Franey slammed the door behind me and locked it."

Nanny shuddered, remembering the metallic smell and the darkness of the coal shed.

"I was in there all day until my mother opened the door that night. She came to get coal to light the fire."

"Why didn't you shout and kick to get out like I did to get out of the sack?" asked Princess Tara.

"I did, and then I fell asleep, and when my mother opened the coal shed door she got the fright of her life. Coal dust had made my hair, face, hands and clothes as black as the pots, and she thought I was a hairy monster," Nanny said.

Princess Tara laughed, which Nanny thought was a little rude since she had just let the Princess escape.

"I like you," Princess Tara said smiling at Nanny, "even though you tried to kidnap me. What's your name?"

"Nanny Reilly, and this is my dog Henry Daly," answered Nanny. "Henry Daly comes everywhere with me now since Ned Franey locked me in the coal shed."

"It sounds to me like Ned Franey is a little bit like King Brian," said the Princess. "He likes to play mean tricks on people."

Princess Tara scratched her head and her crown tipped a little. Then she righted her crown and stood tall and straight. Nanny felt herself sit up a little taller and put her shoulders back. The Princess removed her diamond studded crown and placed it carefully on the grass. She tilted her head to the right, gathered her long red hair over her shoulder, and braided it. She snapped her fingers and a tiny green velvet ribbon appeared in the palm of her hand. She tied a neat bow at the end of her braid, threw her hair back over her shoulder, and then placed her crown back on her head.

Nanny had seen this finger snapping magic before by King Brian at Magandy's Pond, but it still amazed her.

"It's time for us to stop King Brian once and for all. We have to make a plan so he won't play any more mean tricks on anyone." She paused and then said, "I have an idea. Here's what we should do."

CHAPTER FOUR

"Let's hurry, Henry Daly," said Nanny, "it's almost dawn. We need to get back to Magandy's Pond. Nanny made it back to King Brian in time. She had the sack over her shoulder.

"Well now," said King Brian, "you made it. I hope for your sake you didn't look in the sack."

I surely didn't," answered Nanny "Here's your rabbit, may I go home now? My mother will be calling me for breakfast in a couple of hours, and I won't be in my bed. She'll be terribly worried and wondering if Ned Franey locked me in the coal shed again."

"Not so fast there, Nanny Reilly," said King Brian, "I have to make sure you brought me the right rabbit. If you didn't, then with a click of my fingers, I'll make the biggest mushroom you ever saw grow on top of that head of yours." King Brian slowly opened the sack. He peeped inside, and a broad smile came across his face. He saw Princess Tara curled up asleep in her pink pajamas. "You did well, Lass. This is the right rabbit all right, and a beautiful rabbit she is too. Be off with you now, and never touch another mushroom in Coolrainy," said King Brian. He carefully tucked the sack under his arm as he ushered Nanny away with the back of his hand while taking several steps towards her. "Off, home with you now before I change my mind." He pointed in the direction of Nanny's house and then turned away from her. King Brian kicked up his heels. He was so elated his body wriggled with delight.

"I'm not going home until you grant me my wish," demanded Nanny, standing with her hands on her hips. "You told me if I brought you back that sack, you would give me one wish. I want my wish."

"Sure, you're a smarter lass than I thought you were," smiled King Brian as he turned back to face Nanny. "What kind of a wish would a young lady like yourself be wanting?"

"My big brother told me that leprechauns can dance jigs all day and night and never get tired. Is that true?" asked Nanny.

"It surely is true," answered King Brian. "Leprechauns are the greatest dancers Ireland has ever known, and sure I'm the greatest dancer leprechauns have ever known."

"Are you able to do the Darby O'Gill two-step?" asked Nanny. "Indeed I am Lass. Sure, that's the finest step in the whole of Ireland, didn't I create it myself? I danced it for the first time when I was a young lad in my new hornpipe shoes, at the Leprechaun's dance and music festival in Ballyconniger. I out stepped the whole lot of them. Sure, I was the pride of Coolrainy." answered King Brian proudly.

"My wish then," said Nanny, "is for you to teach me the Darby O'Gill two step."

"That's a fine choice of a dance, Lass. Stand back there now and give me some room." King Brian gave Nanny a demonstration. "Stand up tall with your shoulders back and your chin up. Look straight ahead of yourself. Right foot, left foot. One, two … one, two, three. One, two … one, two, three. Are you following me?" He glanced at Nanny. "This is a serious matter Nanny Reilly. After all, I have my dancing reputation to think of." He straightened out his cloak and gently placed his hands on both sides of his crown making sure it sat perfectly on his head. He inhaled and looked straight ahead. "One, two … one, two, three. Get your feet well up off the ground and move forward. Dance, dance … one, two, three. Dance, dance … one, two, three." King Brian laid the sack on the ground. He pulled a tin whistle out from under his cloak. He started playing the tin whistle and tapping his foot. Then he took off dancing a jig all around Magandy's Pond.

"I think I know how to do it now," said Nanny. "Follow me and see if I'm doing it right." Nanny started lifting her knees up "One, two … one, two, three. One, two … one, two, three, Dance, dance … one, two, three. Dance, dance … one, two, three." Nanny imitated the King, as she danced around Magandy's Pond.

King Brian followed her, playing his tin whistle and doing the Darby O'Gill two-step. Henry Daly was trotting close behind keeping both Nanny and King Brian in his sights. While Nanny and King Brian were dancing around Magandy's Pond, Princess Tara slipped out of the sack. She was just pretending to be asleep. She hid behind a mushroom and watched the dancing.

"Hold it there, Lass," said King Brian. "Sure, you're not doing it right. Never let it be said that King Brian, king of all the leprechauns in Coolrainy, couldn't teach a young lady the Darby O'Gill two-step. We leprechauns take pride in our dancing." King Brian put his tin whistle back in his cloak pocket and took out his small shillelagh. "Take a hold of the other end of this shillelagh and stay close to me," he said. "Now on the count of three, start off with your right foot and then do what I do."

"All right," said Nanny, holding the other end of the shillelagh, "but can we dance around the field instead of the pond? I don't want to slip and fall into Magandy's Pond. My brother told me it could take weeks to get back from Australia, it's that far down."

King Brian laughed. "It's a strange lass you are, Nanny Reilly, but it's your wish. C'mon over here, and I'll turn you into the second best dancer in the whole of Ireland," he said.

Nanny and King Brian took off dancing around the field. The King was laughing and thoroughly enjoying himself. Now his sullen green eyes sparkled and he began singing in his lovely tenor voice.

"Dance, dance, wherever you may be.
I am the Lord of the dance said he.
And I lead you all wherever you may be,
And I lead you all to the dance said he."

"Now, follow me again and see if I'm doing it right," laughed Nanny. She was having fun dancing the Darby O'Gill two-step in the cool almost dawn. King Brian followed Nanny Reilly around the field and down the bog road. Nanny knew he would be so involved in the intricate steps, he wouldn't be paying attention to where they were headed. Princess Tara jumped up on Henry Daly's back, and they followed Nanny and King Brian.

CHAPTER FIVE

They danced across Clancy's footbridge. Tom the plough horse was back at his resting spot behind the leafy oak tree. He raised his head and pricked his ears. This time he didn't run in fright. King Brian and Nanny came dancing through in high gear. Nanny looked at Tom and again put her finger to her lips reminding him not to tell anyone. Tom twitched his ears back and forth and nickered.

They danced their way up the ferny trail on Sarah's hill. Nanny was beginning to get tired as the made their way down to O'Brien's Half-acre. After all, she'd already had a hike that very night. She glanced behind her. Henry Daly was panting a little but still going strong.

Princess Tara gave Nanny a thumbs up sign. She was as fresh as a daisy and well rested.

Small beads of sweat began trickling down King Brian's forehead. His crown had tilted on his head.

Nanny's headache came back. This was not a good time for King Brian to get tired and to stop dancing. Nanny had to think quickly. King Brian was down to his last note. She began singing her own song hoping it would last long enough. If not, she would repeat the chorus. They always do that in school, every time the class sang songs for the Christmas Holidays and nobody could remember the words.

"Toor a looh, one-two-three
Toor a lay, one-two-three.
Singing toor a lie, toor a lie, toor a lie eh.
We'll dance through the streams,

We'll dance through the meadows.
We'll dance o'er the mountains
We're good dancing fellows
We'll dance through the evening,
We'll dance all night long.
We'll dance 'til tomorrow,
If nothing goes wrong.
Toor a loo, one-two-three,
Toor a lay, one-two-three,
Singing toor a lie, toor a lie, toor a lie eh."

And there they were, at Katie's Field in Ballineskar.

"You're a grand singer, Nanny Reilly," said King Brian as he huffed and puffed and mopped his forehead with a green handkerchief. "And I'd never think that to look at you. Sure, you're full of surprises."

Nanny thought how right he was.

"This is the most dancing I've done since St. Patrick's Day," laughed King Brian. "You've got it now, Lass. I'll give you credit for being a good dancer. Sure you're as good as any leprechaun I know. Now you'll be able to teach anyone the Darby O'Gill two-step and be ready for St. Patrick's Day next year. Remember to tell everybody that King Brian, king of all the leprechauns of Coolrainy, gave you the dancing lessons." He brushed the lapel of his checkered waistcoat with the tips of his fingers, then held his waistcoat at the waist and tugged on it. He bowed low and when he stood up straight, Nanny laughed out loud.

"I'll be sure to tell them all about you, King Brian," said Nanny Reilly, still giggling. "You're the leprechaun with ears like a rabbit." Nanny moved her hands up above her head as if she had tall, slim rabbit ears.

"Ears like a rabbit?" said King Brian. He grabbed his ears. "Saints preserve me, my ears are long and furry. Look at my hands! They look like rabbit paws, and I can feel whiskers on my face. What's after happening to me? You tricked me."

"Yes I did," said Nanny with her hands on her hips, "because you tricked me." "How did you know I love to dance, and how did you know I would turn into a

rabbit if I stepped foot in Ballineskar?" cried King Brian.

With that, Henry Daly walked up with Princess Tara on his back, stood beside Nanny, and sniffed in a patronizing way.

"I told her," Princess Tara said, sitting up straight on Henry Daly's back. "You tricked Nanny Reilly into kidnapping me so you could ransom me for the crock of gold. Then you would be King of Ballineskar and play mean tricks on the people and leprechauns of Ballineskar again. You're a mean leprechaun, Uncle Brian," the Princess said, shaking her finger at her rabbit-eared uncle.

"You're supposed to be nice to people and grant them three wishes." She held up three fingers and shook her hand for emphasis

"Three wishes?" Nanny said, crossing her arms over her chest. "I only got one wish." She took a step toward King Brian. "You owe me two more wishes."

"Indeed I do," answered King Brian, "but I have no power now. I'm a rabbit. You could try wishing me back to Magandy's Pond, then I might be able to come up with another wish for you."

"Don't listen to a word he says, Nanny Reilly," the little Princess said. "He's only trying to trick you again. If you wish him back to Magandy's Pond, he'll find another way to kidnap me, and he might make a mushroom grow out of your head." Princess Tara swung her leg over Henry's back and dismounted. She tossed her long red braid over her shoulder and marched towards King Brian swinging her arms with each stride. She stopped inches away from him placed her hands on her hips, glared at him and said, "The only way anyone is safe from Uncle Brian is to leave him as a rabbit until he swears by all the saints and scholars of Ireland that he'll never play a mean trick on anybody ever again," Then she about turned and marched back to Henry Daly. Henry gave a quick bark and a growl at King Brian telling him to stay right there.

"Why don't you swear on all the saints and scholars of Ireland?" asked Nanny. "Then you won't be a rabbit anymore."

"Because I have a lot of fun playing tricks on everybody," King Brian said. "I don't think they're mean. They're fun." He blushed slightly and Nanny didn't know if it was embarrassment or just all that dancing. The King continued, "if I break my promise to all the saints and scholars of Ireland, I'll never be able to dance again, and I'll have to live on my own down at Ravens Point. I'll never see another leprechaun or human being for ever, and ever."

"That's a long time," agreed Nanny. "Well, then you should make a promise and keep it. You don't have to play mean tricks on anybody. You can play fun tricks on them instead. And I know you know the difference between mean tricks and fun tricks, King Brian."

Nanny smiled remembering her brother Frank's trick. "My brother played a fun trick on me on Christmas Day. He pretended he was Santa Claus and gave me a cowboy hat like Annie Oakley's and new collar for Henry Daly."

"I think you have me there, Lass," answered King Brian. "I never thought of playing fun tricks on anyone." King Brian's face softened and he bowed his head. He sighed, realizing perhaps his sense of humor could use a little adjusting.

"I'm going to make a promise, this very moment, on all the saints and scholars of Ireland that I will never play a mean trick on anyone ever again." He put his left hand on his heart and raised his right hand in the air.

At that very moment, there was a gust of wind, and the rabbit ears and whiskers disappeared. King Brian looked just like himself again. Except this time his face was not sinister, it was a kind face. His green eyes were not sullen or cloudy, they were smiling and bright. His body was not cock-of-the-walk, it was relaxed and friendly.

Princess Tara was very happy, and so was Nanny. Now she knew for sure King Brian wasn't going to make a mushroom grow out of her head.

King Brian lifted Princess Tara up in the air and said "I know you're only eight inches tall, and it's a bit of a stretch for me to bend down and pick you up, but you're worth the stretch. You may be small on the outside but you're as big as a mountain on the inside. You are grand lass. Your parents will be very proud of you."

Then King Brian turned to Nanny and said, "I think you have two more wishes, Nanny Reilly. What is your second wish?"

Nanny did not have to think too hard for the second wish. "I wish Ned Franey would leave me and everybody else alone and not play any more mean tricks on us."

"Done," laughed King Brian. "You're a good lass too, Nanny Reilly. You deserve the biggest of wishes to come true." King Brian straightened his crown, spat into the palms of his hands, and rubbed them together. "Give me your best shot Nanny Reilly. What is your third wish?"

Nanny thought hard for a moment. She didn't know what else to wish for once Ned Franey was going to leave her alone. She looked at Henry Daly. She loved her dog. He was her very best friend in the whole, wide world.

"I know what to wish for," said Nanny. She knelt beside Henry Daly, patted him on the head, hugged him and said, "I wish Henry Daly could talk"

"Done," said King Brian.

"Can Henry Daly really talk, King Brian?" asked Nanny.

"Of course he can!" replied King Brian. "Ask him anything you like."

Nanny looked her best friend squarely in the eye. "How old are you, Henry Daly?" Nanny held her breath and waited.

Henry Daly looked right back at her with his ears pricked forward. "I'm six and a half years old," answered Henry Daly in a barky-sounding voice. "Holy, moley!" said Henry, his doggy mouth curled into a smile. "I can talk!"

"You surely can!" said Nanny in astonishment. "Say something else!"

"What will I say?" asked Henry Daly. He turned around in a circle, like he was chasing his tail. Then he stopped and said, "I do that when I'm happy, Nanny Reilly."

"I thought you turned in a circle when you're happy, Henry Daly, but now I know for sure." Nanny Reilly laughed into the cool morning air. She wrapped her arms around Henry Daly and hugged him tightly. "Jeepers, I never heard a dog talk before."

"Well, you better get used to it Lass," laughed King Brian. "But you don't want him talking to everybody. Keep it to yourself or the whole village will follow you everywhere you go, and they won't leave Henry Daly alone. Off home with you now, Nanny Reilly, it's almost dawn. And don't forget," King Brian put his finger to his lips, "it's a secret about Henry Daly."

CHAPTER SIX

King Brian and Princess Tara invited Nanny and Henry Daly back on midsummer's eve. It was going to be the biggest leprechaun dance in the whole country. All the leprechauns from two provinces would be there, and they would all be dancing until dawn.

Nanny said goodbye to King Brian and Princess Tara. She told them herself and Henry Daly would love to come back on midsummer's eve. She and Henry Daly ran off home with their new secret chatting all the way.

"Get yourself cleaned up Nanny," said her mother, "we're going into town. We need to do some shopping. I promised Mrs. Franey we would take her and Ned with us today because Ned needs to get new shoes. Henry will have to stay at home, there's no room in the car for him today."

"But Henry Daly always comes to town with us. Why can't Ned Franey stay at home?" cried Nanny.

"Saints preserve you, Nanny Reilly. I'll have to wash your mouth out with soap," said Nanny's mother. "It's only right to give people a helping hand when they need it."

Nanny felt a little ashamed and didn't say another word. She remembered her brother telling her that one time, Tommy Riordan's mother washed his mouth out with soap and Tommy was blowing bubbles from his ears for two weeks.

"Ned Franey is coming to town with us today, Henry Daly," said Nanny sadly. "There's no room for you so you'll have to stay at home."

"But what about me?" whimpered Henry Daly. "I always go to town with you to get my bone from Kelly's butcher shop."

Now Nanny Reilly felt twice as unhappy. She had to sacrifice a day with her devoted pal for a day with her archenemy Ned Franey.

"I'll get your bone from Mr. Kelly for you," Nanny told Henry Daly.

"But that doesn't make me feel any better," answered Henry. He dropped his head and tail and walked away from Nanny.

"Please don't be sad, Henry Daly," said Nanny. "You know if I could bring you, I would."

"But you can take me with you!" answered Henry. "You can hide me in the back seat of the car and cover me with a blanket. No one will see me."

Nanny Reilly thought for a moment. "OK, but you have to be as quiet as a mouse," Nanny said. "If Ned Franey hears you, he will surely tell on me. He told the teacher on Joey Howlin when he hid the chalk, and Joey had to write out, *I will never hide teacher's chalk again*, in his best handwriting."

Nanny took the top blanket from her bed, then went to her bedroom door and peeked out. First one way, then the other. Her curls tossed themselves from side to side, as she looked both ways. Nanny's mother was double-checking her shopping list and going through her kitchen cabinets, she didn't want to forget anything. Town was a long way away and she only did this trip once a week. Nanny was watching her mother to make sure she couldn't see her. Then Nanny went out to the car with the blanket in her arms, followed closely by Henry Daly. She opened the back door of their ten-year-old gray ford, and Henry Daly jumped in.

"Keep your head down Henry Daly," said Nanny as she covered him up with her blanket, "and whatever you do don't let Ned Franey find you."

"Don't worry Nanny," said Henry, I'll keep quiet, no one will ever know I'm here."

CHAPTER SEVEN

Nanny's mother drove up outside the Franey's house and honked the horn. Ned came running out. His red hair was damp with a sharp crease and neatly combed. He wore a nice blue sweater and blue jeans. He looked tidier and happier than Nanny had ever seen him.

"Hello, Nanny Reilly," he said with the brightest smile on his face. "Where's Henry Daly?"

Nanny was stunned. "Ned Franey has a smile on his face, and he's being nice to me," thought Nanny. "My second wish came true, too!"

"Eh, Henry Daly had to stay at home. There wasn't enough room," answered Nanny. "But I promised him I would get him a bone from Mr. Kelly, the butcher."

"Is he waiting at home for his bone? asked Ned.

"Yes he is waiting at home, he's guarding the house while we shop," answered Nanny. She looked down at the blanket. Henry was as quiet as he had promised to be. He never moved a muscle.

"May I play with you and Henry Daly tomorrow?" asked Ned as he climbed into the back of the car beside Nanny. Henry Daly was well hidden to Nanny's left, and Ned sat to her right.

"If you like," said Nanny. "We'll be picking blackberries tomorrow. I know where the biggest blackberries in Coolrainy are. My brother told me you need buckets as big as elephant's feet to fit all the blackberries in, there so big."

Nanny and Ned chatted the whole way into town. Though she'd have never believed it, Ned became her friend. When they got to town, their mothers told them to wait in the car while they went to the bank.

Nanny Reilly was a little on edge. She wanted to let Henry Daly out of the car.

Nanny looked at the blanket and patted it, and then she looked back at Ned. "Can you keep a secret?" she asked Ned.

"Sure I can," answered Ned. "What is it?"

"Henry Daly is hiding under this blanket. My mother told me to leave him at home because there was no room, but Henry Daly wanted to come with us. It was his idea to hide under a blanket." Nanny wished she hadn't said that.

"It was his idea? quizzed Ned, "What do you mean?"

"Eh, I mean he ran to the car with a blanket when I told him he had to stay at home," answered Nanny.

"I didn't know Henry Daly was so clever," said Ned, "how did he know to hide under a blanket?"

"Jeepers," said Nanny Reilly. "Can you keep another secret?"

"I surely can. What secret do you have? I love secrets!" answered Ned excitedly. Ned looked over both his shoulders and rolled up the car window. His blue eyes widened and a broad smile crossed his freckled face.

"First I have to let Henry Daly out of the car. Then he'll show you," replied Nanny. She opened the car door. Henry tossed off the blanket, jumped out, and shook himself off. Nanny could tell by Henry Daly's doggie smile that he was happy to get out and stretch his legs.

"Henry Daly, tell Ned how old you are." Nanny asked.

"I'm six and a half years old," answered Henry.

"Wow!" Said Ned. "How did Henry Daly learn to talk?"

Nanny told Ned all about her three wishes from King Brian at Magandy's Pond. She told him how she was tricked into kidnapping Princess Tara. Now King Brian and Princess Tara were her friends, and she had been invited to the leprechauns dance at midnight on midsummer's eve.

"May I go to the dance with you?" asked Ned, "I've never seen a leprechaun before. I promise to keep your secret. I won't tell anybody."

"Sure you can," Nanny replied, "I can teach you the Darby O'Gill two-step."

"Thank you, Nanny Reilly," said Ned. "I was so mean to you many times, but I promise you I will never be mean to you or anyone else again. I will be your friend from now on."

Nanny was so pleased to hear Ned say that. She was happy to have Ned as her friend.

Before Nanny and Ned's mothers came back, Henry Daly jumped into the car under the blanket to hide out again. Ned went shopping with his mother to pick out his new shoes, and Nanny Reilly and her mother did their weekly grocery shopping, not forgetting Henry Daly's bone from Mr. Kelly's butcher shop.

CHAPTER EIGHT

On midsummer's eve, Nanny and Ned went to bed at their regular bedtime. Once everybody was asleep, they got out of bed and dressed up in their Sunday best for the dance. Nanny Reilly wore her cowgirl hat, Henry Daly wore his nice collar, and Ned wore his new shoes. Nanny arranged to meet Ned at the cross at ten minutes to midnight. Then they would make their way to Magandy's Pond with Henry Daly on guard at their side.

"This is where I met King Brian the last time," Nanny told Ned as they approached the mushroom King Brian had sat on to trick Nanny. Before Nanny could say another word, she heard that familiar voice.

"Well Nanny Reilly, it is a pleasure to have a fine dancer like yourself attend our midsummer's eve dance. We welcome you and your new friend, Ned, to our shindig. This is a night of celebration for leprechauns all over Ireland. We're celebrating all our good fortune. Yourself, Henry Daly and Ned are our guests of honor."

King Brian's regalia, was the insignia of kingship. His cloak was a dark rich and royal green. The borders were lined with emeralds and solid gold studs. He clapped his hands three times. Music filled the air, and out of a rabbit's burrow beside Magandy's Pond came one thousand leprechauns wearing splendid green and gold clothing, dancing the Darby O'Gill two-step. King Brian clapped his hands three more times, and fifty leprechauns wearing aprons over their splendid attire came dancing out of the burrow with all kinds of food on big silver platters. They even had a platter full of big, juicy bones for Henry Daly. Then one more time King Brian clapped his hands three times, and fifty more leprechauns came dancing out with jugs full of all kinds of drinks. What a feast it was. Nanny and Ned looked at each other in awe. They were mesmerized by the thousand tiny leprechauns dancing, and never before had they seen so much food.

"Wow!" said Ned excitedly. "This is better than the Coolrainy fair. Thank you, Nanny Reilly, for allowing me come to the dance with you."

"You and Henry Daly are my very best friends," replied Nanny. "Come on Ned, let me teach you the Darby O'Gill two-step. This is the best dance in the whole of Ireland." Nanny and Ned went two-stepping among the leprechauns, and Henry Daly feasted on his silver platter of juicy bones. What a great time they were having. After a half hour of dancing, Nanny and Ned felt hungry and thirsty, so they decided to join Henry Daly feasting. King Brian was not dancing. Nanny noticed him standing on top of a large mushroom, looking out over the fields.

"Where's Princess Tara?" asked Nanny "I thought she was going to be here."

"I'm wondering that myself, Lass." answered King Brian. "Never before has a leprechaun been late for the midsummer's eve dance, especially a leprechaun King from one of the provinces. I've sent one of my best leprechaun scouts over to Ballineskar to find out what the delay is and if there is anything I can do? I'm a little bit concerned."

"What's that noise I hear in the distance?" asked Ned.

"Stop the music" yelled King Brian. "Stop the music." The music suddenly stopped. The only sound that could be heard was the faraway sound of a horn. "That noise you hear in the distance," said King Brian, "is the leprechaun's distress horn. Something is terribly wrong."

King Brian reached into his cloak and pulled out a bugle. He blew the bugle once and yelled out, "All leprechaun soldiers report for duty"

More than six hundred leprechauns ran back into the burrow they had come dancing out of. Two minutes later they came charging out on miniature horses. The lead leprechaun soldier was leading a white horse for King Brian. The King mounted his horse. He then turned to Nanny and Ned and said, "You two should go home and stay there. We don't know what trouble is out there, and you need to be safe. Stay close to Nanny Reilly and Ned on their way home Henry Daly. Guard them well."

"But maybe we can help," said Nanny.

"Yeah," said Ned. "We're strong."

"I know you are both strong, and I thank you for your offer of help, but you must be off home now. Henry Daly will take good care of you both," replied King Brian. With that, King Brian blew his bugle one more time and shouted, "Onward leprechaun soldiers."

King Brian and his leprechaun army charged off into the night on their miniature horses. They were ready to answer the call of distress.

CHAPTER NINE

"What will we do, Nanny Reilly?" asked Ned, as he watched the army of leprechauns gallop away on their horses. He scratched his head vigorously and in frustration, making a mess of his red hair "Do you think we should follow them or go home?"

Nanny tightened the stampede cord on her cowboy hat. The leprechaun army was almost out of sight. "If Annie Oakley and the Lone Ranger were here, they would follow them. They always save people. I think we should follow them," answered Nanny. "Princess Tara is in trouble, and she's my friend!"

"She's my friend too," said Henry Daly tilting his head to one side with his ears pricked, and blinking his big brown eyes as he looked up at Nanny. "Let's follow them. I can sniff them out."

"When King Brian sees us he'll be mad at us for not going home," said Ned.

"We can stay out of sight hiding behind blackberry bushes, ditches and trees," replied Nanny Reilly.

"Yeah you're right Nanny, let's follow them," agreed Ned.

"Alright then, let's go," said Henry Daly, sniffing the ground and picking up the scent of the leprechaun soldiers. Nanny and Ned bravely marched behind Henry, swinging their arms and looking straight ahead. Left, left, left right left. They marched over Clancy's footbridge. Tom the plough horse was standing under the oak tree at the other side.

"It's only me Tom, Nanny Reilly," said Nanny, "Henry Daly and Ned Franey are with me, don't be afraid."

Tom nickered back at Nanny. He wasn't afraid. He was well used to Nanny Reilly and her entourage going back and forth during the night. It wasn't long before they caught up with King Brian and his army.

"Stay down as low as you can," whispered Henry Daly, "and stay as quiet as a mouse. Listen to what King Brian is saying." Nanny, Ned and Henry Daly skulked behind a sycamore tree.

The leprechaun soldiers were gathered around the trunk of an oak tree in the middle of Katie's field. Beside the rabbit burrow, where Nanny had captured Princess Tara, King Brian was sitting on his white horse, facing his soldiers.

"Leprechaun soldiers of Coolrainy," he shouted. "We don't have much time. We have just found out by our scout that King Rory and Princess Tara were kidnapped by a big burly man. He carried them off in a burlap sack, and we don't know where they are. The identity of the captor is at this time is unknown. I believe he will use Princess Tara to demand the crock of gold from King Rory. They must be found before dawn, or they will be traded to the wicked Banshee of Raven's Point, and disappear forever. My poor brother and lovely niece will join all the other poor leprechaun souls in the Banshee's Cradle. We will never lay eyes on them again. Spread out the whole lot of you."

King Brian cantered his white horse in a small circle holding his shillelagh high in the air. "We'll have to search every nook and cranny in all the surrounding villages, and we've only five hours to do it. We need to spread out as far as we can and track them down." His imperial cloak flowed behind him showing the gold satin lining. Miscellaneous pockets had various items, such as, his tin whistle, his bugle, a green notebook with a gold ribbon marking his most recent entry, and his favorite hornpipe shoes. He wondered if he would get to dance in them tonight, or for that matter, ever again.

The leprechaun soldiers rode away in all directions at a gallop. King Brian held his horse back. He put his shillelagh back in his cloak. He removed his crown, held it against his heart and looked up to the heavens.

"I have to find my brother and my niece before dawn or that's surely the end of them," he said softly. He knew the Banshee was a mean old witch, and she was out every night until dawn searching for victims to work in her Dreary Castle, in the Banshee's Cradle. If a soul didn't escape her grasp by dawn, they were never seen again. He bowed his head. His white horse stood perfectly still and shined in the full moonlight of midsummer's eve. "I would sacrifice myself and all I possess to save them from the Banshee's Cradle." His tears fell to the loamy earth, and they too shined in the moonlight.

Nanny, Ned and Henry Daly were still hiding behind the sycamore tree. They heard every word King Brian said. They stood quietly just watching him until he rode away. They now knew what a scared King Brian looked like.

"The Banshee's Cradle," said Ned, breaking the silence.

"Now what do we do?" said Nanny. "I'm afraid of the Banshee."

"I have an idea," exclaimed Henry Daly. "I can go down into Princess Tara's burrow, take something that belongs to her and get her scent. Once I have her scent, I can track her down and find her and King Rory before dawn."

Nanny and Ned were excited about Henry's idea. Henry Daly crawled down into the burrow. Less than a minute later, he crawled back out carrying Princess Tara's pink pajamas with the tiny shamrocks on them in his mouth. He zigzagged around Katie's field sniffing out the scent.

"I got it," yelled Henry Daly. "The scent is over here."

"Find them, Henry Daly, find them." Nanny Reilly cried.

"Good boy, Henry Daly. You're a great dog. Lead us to them," Ned shouted.

Henry took off running to the end of the field. The scent took him through a gate and into a lane. He followed the lane to the end. He came to another gate. On the other side of the gate was a small cottage with a couple of old sheds surrounded by large sycamore trees. There was a light on in the house, and they could see a figure passing the window.

"They're in there," whispered Henry Daly. "We'll have to find a way to get them out."

"That's Bull Cullen's house," said Nanny. "Everybody calls him Bull because he's mean. He's always chasing us out of Katie's Field. My brother told me to be careful of that fellah. He said Bull Cullen waits for children to go into Katie's Field and throws a fishing net over them to catch them."

"We have to be very quiet," Nanny whispered. "You go first, Henry Daly."

With careful steps on the soft ground, Henry Daly led Nanny and Ned to the window of the cottage. They were careful not to make a sound. All three of them peeked in the window. They could see Bull Cullen opening a sack. They were sure King Rory and Princess Tara were in it, but there was no movement from the sack at all. Nanny remembered how Princess Tara had kicked with all her might when she had her in the sack.

Bull Cullen just looked into the sack, smiled, and closed it up again. He left the sack sitting on the table while he stoked the fire and poured himself a cup of steaming hot tea. He kicked his big old heavy shoes off and sat in a rocking chair beside the fire, keeping a watchful eye on his burlap sack.

"Why isn't Princess Tara kicking the sack?" whispered Nanny. "Henry Daly, do you remember when I captured her, she kicked so hard she bruised my back?"

"I do," said Henry, "and she was doing a lot of shouting at you, too."

"Do you think they are already gone to the Banshee's Cradle?" asked Ned.

"I hope not," replied Nanny. "We need to get that sack." Nanny turned from the window and scanned Bull Cullen's yard. She glanced up at the mighty sycamore tree shading his cottage. She tightened the stampede cord on her cowboy hat. "I have an idea, follow me," she said.

Henry Daly and Ned followed Nanny Reilly to one of the old sheds.

Nanny whispered, "Look around for Bull Cullen's fishing nets and some rope. He must keep them somewhere around here." "We'll climb the tree and get him to come out of the house. Then we'll throw the net over him and tie him up."

"But he's too big for us, Nanny Reilly," said Ned "We need to knock him to the ground first, and we have to be quick about it or he'll catch us and we'll end up as his Sunday dinner."

"You're right," said Nanny. "We need to think of something fast."

"I know," said Henry Daly. "We need a trip rope, too!"

"A trip rope! Why?" asked Ned.

"We can tie it across his footpath to trip him up," said Henry. "Then you'll be able to get the net over him."

"I'll knock the door and run," said Nanny. "Bull Cullen will run after me and trip over the rope! You're so clever, Henry Daly!" continued Nanny Reilly as she put her arms around her pal.

"You're smarter than any other dog I know," added Ned, "and you can talk too!"

Nanny could feel her tummy fill with butterflies. This was scary. But the image of her little leprechaun princess friend gave her courage.

Nanny and Ned quietly arranged the trip rope about ten yards from the front door while Henry Daly kept a watchful eye on Bull Cullen through the window. Then they both climbed the big sycamore tree that leaned over the footpath. They placed the fishing net on two large limbs a couple of feet apart, directly above where Bull Cullen was going to fall. After the net was placed in position, Nanny jumped down from the tree and Ned remained in the tree. Nanny signaled to Henry Daly that they were ready to carry out their plan.

"OK, Henry Daly," whispered Nanny. "We're ready."

CHAPTER TEN

Nanny slipped up to the front door of Bull Cullen's house. She turned and looked up in the tree at Ned and gave him a thumbs up. Knock! Knock! Knock! Nanny pounded on the door. She dashed to the other side of the trip rope. Nothing happened. The door didn't open. "He's not coming out," Nanny whispered, her voice concerned.

Ned was squatting in the tree waiting to drop the net on Bull Cullen. "Maybe he didn't hear you. Knock again," Ned whispered. "Can you see him, Henry Daly? What's he doing?"

Henry was still watching Bull Cullen through the window. "He's hiding the sack behind his rocking chair. Here he comes," whispered Henry Daly. "Get Ready!"

Nanny and Ned were scared. This was worse than any scary movie, and it was too late to change their minds. The cottage door swung open wide. Bull Cullen filled the whole doorway.

"Who's out there at this unholy hour?" he shouted, his voice rumbling into the night. He took a step forward and saw Nanny. I'll catch you Nanny Reilly!" he roared. "Then I'll eat you for supper!" He took off running after Nanny.

Nanny bolted toward the gate. Bull Cullen took long strides and covered a lot of ground. Ned was ready with the net. Henry Daly darted into the house to grab the sack.

"Come back here!" Bull shouted at Nanny. He didn't see the trip rope. His right foot got caught and pulled Bull Cullen's big bulky body to a screeching halt. Both his arms stretched out in front of him. His mouth and eyes were wide open as he crashed to the concrete footpath face down. "Ouch what happened?" He yelled.

Ned let the net go and it landed perfectly over Bull Cullen. "Come on, quickly, Nanny," shouted Ned as he jumped out of the tree and landed on Bull. "Grab the rope!"

Nanny snatched the rope and tried with all her might to tie up Bull Cullen. But the big man twisted and turned, and he was very strong. He was making brave attempts to stand and remove the fishing net.

"I'll tear the hides off the two of you!" roared Bull. He put his big hands on one rope and pulled hard.

"He's getting loose!" Nanny cried out to Ned, as the angry man's grimace changed to an evil grin. He grabbed Nanny Reilly by the ankle and pulled her down. She kicked and screamed to get free. Ned was doing everything he could to help Nanny but Bull had grabbed his ankle, too.

"I'll tear the hide off you!" growled an angry voice. "Let them go or I'll have you for supper!" Nanny and Ned looked up in shock. That was the angriest voice they had ever heard. Who could it be?

Henry Daly was standing nose-to-nose with Bull Cullen snarling— his sharp, wolf-like teeth gleamed in the moonlight. His eyes were fierce; saliva dripped from his mouth, and the hackles on his neck and back stood up like spikes. "Stay where you are and let them go!" growled Henry Daly.

With a flick of his wrist, Bull let Nanny and Ned go. "I'm not going to hurt them," he told Henry Daly in a soft, shaky voice. "Look, I'm letting them go. Sure, there's no harm done."

Bull turned his head and lay face down on the footpath with the fishing net over his head, neck, and shoulders. He didn't want to see Henry Daly's dripping saliva. He was praying that fierce mad dog would go away. Henry's face was one inch from Bull's face. Nanny and Ned quickly stood and backed toward the gate, keeping their attention on the defeated Bull Cullen. When they got to the gate, they turned and high tailed it back down the lane as fast as their legs would carry them. Nanny's stampede cord was down on her neck, her cowboy hat blew in the wind, and her auburn curls bounced off her head every stride she took. Ned's red hair was straight up off his forehead and blowing back in the wind. His new shoes took him down the lane ten strides ahead of Nanny.

"Did you hear Henry Daly?" said Nanny gasping for breath, when they had secured a safe distance between themselves and Bull Cullen.

"I surely did!" exclaimed Ned huffing and puffing as he rested bent over with both hands on his knees "Did you see Henry's teeth? I was afraid of him myself. Just the look of him scared me."

"I never knew he could look so angry," replied Nanny placing her hat back on her head and tightening her stampede cord. "He sure scared Bull Cullen. I thought we were doomed."

"Yeah, me too!" answered Ned. "I was sure we were going to be Bull Cullen's Sunday supper."

"Look!" cried Nanny, pointing up the lane. "Here comes Henry Daly, and he has the sack." Henry bounded toward them.

"What a dog!" said Ned. "He's the greatest."

Henry laid the sack at Nanny Reilly's feet.

"There's still no sign of life," said Henry quietly. Nanny pulled opened the drawstring of the sack and looked inside. King Rory and Princess Tara appeared to be sleeping. Princess Tara had both her hands joined together under her left cheek and she had her knees curled up to her chest. Her head was tucked in to one corner of the sack and the little Princess was breathing softly. King Rory was sitting in the other corner of the sack with his head tilted to one side and his crown down on his nose. He was snoring quietly.

CHAPTER ELEVEN

The tiny Princess looked so peaceful. Nanny put her finger in the sack and touched the Princess Tara's small cheek. "Wake up, Princess Tara. It's me, Nanny Reilly." Nanny said quietly.

Princess Tara opened her eyes and looked up at Nanny Reilly. She stretched her arms wide just as if she were wakening up from a good night's sleep.

King Rory then opened his eyes. "Saints preserve the lot of us," he said. "Are we safe?"

"Yes, Father, we're safe," answered Princess Tara. "My friend Nanny Reilly saved us."

"I didn't do it alone," said Nanny. "Henry Daly and my best friend Ned Franey helped me."

"Sure you are the two bravest young children in the whole of Ireland," said King Rory. "When that mean man knocked us unconscious, I thought that was the end of everything for us. I was dreaming of the Banshee's Cradle."

"We heard King Brian talking about the Banshee's Cradle." Ned said. "He said you both had to be found before dawn. He and all his leprechaun soldiers are searching the whole of Ballineskar and Coolrainy for you. I thought you were goners!"

"Goners is a good word for it," said King Rory. "Let's find King Brian and let him know we're safe. Your bravery was a blessing for us. I thank you all from the bottom of my heart. You will be rewarded for what you have done for us."

Princess Tara jumped on Henry Daly's back and hugged him tightly, "you too Henry Daly, you're so brave."

Nanny and Ned blushed and got a little bashful. They looked to the ground and twisted their bodies a little. Then they looked at each other smiling. At the time, they didn't realize they were being brave. But when they got over their bashful moment, they realized how brave they were.

King Rory took a horn from his cloak pocket and blew it. It was like the horn King Brian used to blow the distress signal. Except this time the sound was a joyous one. Another horn rang out in the distance, answering the call for celebration.

"Let's go to Coolrainy and continue the midsummer's eve dance. We surely must celebrate our good fortune now," said King Rory.

King Rory joined Princess Tara on Henry Daly's back and the five of them headed back to Magandy's Pond to join all the other leprechauns.

When they got there, King Brian and all the leprechauns were waiting for them. They heard all about the bravery of Nanny Reilly, Ned Franey, and Henry Daly.

King Brian stood on a toadstool and then called for silence. "May I please have everyone's attention? I have a very proud presentation to make to our newfound friends here. He took three tiny gold whistles from his cloak. "Take these whistles and keep them with you at all times. Wherever you go in Ireland you can blow on these whistles, and the leprechaun king of that province will appear and help you with your wishes. From this very moment, you are all as magic as any leprechaun in Ireland."

Nanny's face lit up. "We're magic like leprechauns!" she said looking at Ned.

"That's like being your own genie!" replied Ned

"It sure is!" answered Nanny. "Sure, I don't know what to wish for. May I think for a minute?"

"Take as long as you like," said King Brian. "Your wishes will always be there."

"I wish for another platter of those juicy bones," said Henry Daly, licking his lips.

"Done," said King Brian laughing. A big silver platter of juicy bones appeared in front of Henry Daly.

"Holy moley!" said Henry Daly. "I like this wishing stuff."

"I wish for a cowboy hat like Nanny Reilly's!" wished Ned.

"Done," said King Brian. A cowboy hat exactly like Nanny's appeared on Ned's head.

"I like this wishing stuff, too, Henry Daly." Ned said, removing his new hat to admire it.

"What about yourself, Lass?" King Brian asked Nanny Reilly.

"There's only one wish I want tonight," said Nanny.

"What is the one wish you would like tonight, Nanny Reilly?" asked King Brian.

"I wish Bull Cullen would forget what happened and not be mean anymore," said Nanny. She surely didn't want to run into Bull Cullen again after the events of tonight.

"Done," said King Brian, "and a wise wish it is too."

"Let's dance and celebrate!" said Princess Tara.

"Before we dance, there is one more thing I would like to do," said King Brian

"What's that?" asked Princess Tara.

"A fine young cowgirl and a fine young cowboy, with two fine hats like that, deserve something to go with them," answered King Brian. He clapped his hands three times, and before Nanny and Ned's eyes appeared two ponies. One black, and one white. Nanny chose the white pony, whose name was Frosty. The black pony, Bertie, was Ned's.

CHAPTER TWELVE

It had rained all day and night the day before, and in a seaside village, that was the best time to go beachcombing. And that was just what Nanny and Ned wanted to do on this particular day. Now they had their new ponies to ride, and their cowboy hats to wear, they could finally go to Raven's Point, where all the treasures from all the shipwrecks were.

"My brother told me that Long John Silver is buried at Raven's Point, and his wooden leg is still floating in the Atlantic Ocean with his parrot sitting on it," said Nanny Reilly as she and Ned rode Bertie and Frosty down the Bog Road to the beach. Henry Daly trotted along behind them.

"Maybe the treasure is buried with him," said Ned. "My mother said old Mrs. Boyle asked that all her treasures get buried with her."

"We can dig up the buried treasure!" said Nanny excitedly.

"Yeah," said Ned "Then we can bury it again in a different place!"

"We can bury it behind the coal shed!" said Nanny. "Nobody but Henry Daly ever goes there."

"Then Henry Daly will be able to guard it for us so no one will steal it from us!" added Ned as Bertie moved from a walk to a trot.

Nanny squeezed Frosty to catch up. Both ponies were trotting side by side at the waters edge. Henry Daly picked up the pace too and bounded his way into the ocean. He wanted to swim a little. Nanny directed Frosty into the ocean behind Henry. The water came up to Frosty's knees as she raised her legs higher with her tail in the air.

"Wait for me Nanny Reilly," said Ned, he asked Bertie to follow. "This is so much fun. I'm really happy to have my pony." Ned looked at Nanny with a broad grin on his face. "I'll race you to the sand dunes. You can go first because you and Frosty are girls."

Nanny didn't answer Ned, she just grinned back at him. In an instant she tightened the stampede cord on her hat, leaned forward, held on to Frosty's mane and the reins at the same time.

"Yeah! yelled Nanny. Frosty was on her toes and ready to oblige. She sprang forward, leaping her way out of the ocean with her tail still in the air. This was a lot of fun for Frosty. She sprayed Ned and Bertie with the ocean water on her way. Ned wasn't quite as ready as Bertie for Nanny's quick departure. He lost his seat a little and found himself grabbing the mane and pulling himself forward to avoid slipping from Bertie's back. He didn't have any time to tighten the stampede cord on his hat, so he had to hold his hat down with one hand, and hold the reins with the other. That's the last time he suggests that girls go first he thought to himself.

Nanny and Frosty reached the sand dunes seconds before Ned and Bertie. Nanny was still wearing her grin.

"OK," said Ned, as he dismounted to give his pony a breather, "you win, but next time we start together." Nanny agreed nodding, as she loosened her stampede cord. She leaned forward and hugged Frosty's neck. Then she slid off her pony's back, took the reins over her head and let her rest a while.

Henry quickly swam his way back to the waters edge. He shook himself off and rolled in the dry sand. He loved the beach. He could see Nanny and Ned sitting in the sand at the foot of the dunes. Bertie and Frosty stood close by grazing on tall reeds. Henry sniffed his way to Nanny and Ned. "Not too many rabbits on the beach," he said, as he shook the sand from his damp body. He dug himself an area in the sand where he could curl up and relax after his swim.

For several minutes, the friends sat and talked about the buried treasure they were going to find. The excitement of it all was almost too much to bear.

"Let's go Nanny Reilly," said Ned, before somebody gets there before us." They both mounted their ponies and headed off trotting towards Ravens Point. Henry Daly led the way.

"Look at the footprints in the sand," said Ned. "Are they coming out of the water?"

"I think they are!" said Nanny. "Maybe it's somebody from a shipwreck."

"Maybe it's a pirate!" said Ned "Let's follow them and see where they go."

"I'll go first," said Henry Daly. Nanny Reilly, Ned Franey, and their ponies followed Henry up the beach to the dunes. The prints went over the dunes and into the forest. Henry followed the scent. Nanny, Ned and their ponies were close behind and feeling a little nervous. The rolling sand dunes leveled out, and small pine trees lined a wide sandy trail. As they rode further down the sandy trail it narrowed and became a grass trail. The trees got taller. Bertie and Frosty snorted. They noticed the change of scenery and felt tension in Nanny and Ned. Soon they made their way a little deeper into the forest. Tall pines surrounded them. Dried twigs littered the trail, and when the ponies trod on them they snapped loudly and the sound carried.

"Do you hear the echo?" asked Ned.

"I do," Nanny said. "It sounds empty in here. I can't hear anything but the twigs breaking. My brother says that when you can hear an echo, it's really the Banshee. Her footsteps make no sound as she floats around and she repeats whatever you say into your ear."

"The Banshee! I heard she only comes out at night," Ned said.

"If she comes after us, Bertie and Frosty will carry us away as fast as lightning, and she'll never catch us!"

Henry Daly came running back. "I found a man behind the trees over there," he said. "I think he's asleep."

"Show us where he is, Henry Daly!" Nanny said. Nanny and Ned rode behind Henry Daly. When they got near to where the man lay, they dismounted, tied Bertie and Frosty to a branch of a fallen tree and slowly crept to him.

The stranger was sleeping soundly with his head resting against the trunk of a pine tree. He wore a brown cap, a thick white woolen sweater, gray trousers and rubber boots.

"Do you think he's a pirate?" whispered Ned.

"No I don't think so." answered Ned. "Sure pirates wear a patch over one eye. Maybe he's a robber and he came this far into the forest to bury the money he robbed."

"Should we wake him up and ask who he is?" Ned asked.

"No," said Nanny, "what if he wakes up and grabs us and we can't get away."

"I'll growl at him," said Henry Daly. "If he grabs me he'll be a sorry man."

Henry took a step toward the sleeping man; he lowered his head and growled. The strange man didn't move.

"Growl again, Henry Daly, he didn't hear you," Nanny said.

Henry took another step forward. His nose was now six inches from the stranger's nose. He growled again. This time his growls were deeper and longer.

The stranger opened his eyes. He saw Henry's stern eyes, long nose and sharp teeth, "I knew it," he mumbled, and then he passed out again.

"I think you scared the life out of him Henry Daly," said Ned.

Henry realized his growling was too severe. He took a few steps back and began barking at the stranger and wagging his tail. Once again, the stranger opened his eyes. Nanny, Ned and Henry Daly stood rigid and stared at him in silence.

The stranger stared back. His eyes shifted from Henry, to Ned, and then to Nanny. "Who are you?" he asked.

"My name is Nanny Reilly," replied Nanny, as she and Ned took a single step back.

"Thank God," the man said relieved. "My name is Fran O'Toole. If I'm here talking to Nanny Reilly, that means I'm still alive, and she didn't get me."

"Who didn't get you?" asked Nanny.

"The Banshee!" said Fran.

"The Banshee!" exclaimed Ned. "Is the Banshee here in the forest? If she is, I want to go home."

"I don't know if she's here. All I know is we were out fishing when a storm came up, and a mighty wave turned our fishing boat over. Mike and I were trying to keep our heads above water when I heard a howl like I'd never heard before."

"Let's get out of here," said Nanny tightening her stampede cord on her cowboy hat. She quickly turned and made her way towards Frosty who was gorging on the fresh green grass around the fallen pine tree she and Bertie were tethered to. Ned tightened the stampede cord on his hat too. This meant they were planning to ride like the wind.

"You can ride my pony, and I'll ride with Ned," a frightened Nanny told Fran O'Toole.

"We can't go yet," said Fran. "We have to look for my friend Mike Donovan. I saw the Banshee lift him up out of the water, and she was laughing like mad at me. She said, don't go anywhere, I'll be back for you! Then she took him off in this direction."

"I'm scared," said Ned. "Can we go?"

"If you two want to go, don't let me stop you." Fran said. "I have to find Mike before I go anywhere. There's no time to go looking for help. It could take hours for anyone to get here."

"I know who can help!" exclaimed Nanny. "King Brian!"

"Yeah!" cried Ned. "King Brian can help!"

"King Brian, who's that?" Fran asked.

"He's the king of all the leprechauns of all Coolrainy," said Nanny. "If I blow my whistle, he'll show up and give me a wish." Nanny pulled her new gold whistle from the pocket of her blue jeans.

"I don't have time for your jokes right now," Fran said angrily. "Go home, the pair of you, and leave me alone. I'll find Mike without you." Fran got to his feet and dusted the pine needles off his trousers. "Whoever heard of such a ridiculous thing? King Brian my eye," he added.

"It's true!" Ned said in Nanny's defense. "He gave me this cowboy hat, and he gave Henry Daly some juicy bones."

"He gave us our ponies, and then he made Henry Daly talk," added Nanny, hoping she sounded convincing to poor Fran. She could imagine how her story sounded to anyone, and especially to someone who'd been attacked by the Banshee.

"Who's Henry Daly?" Fran asked.

"My dog," said Nanny.

"That's it. I've heard enough!" Fran said angrily as he straightened his hat. "The two of you get up on your magic ponies and take your talking dog with you." He shook his fist at them and said, "Get out of here, the pair of you, and don't say another word." Fran O'Toole marched off, leaving Nanny and Ned speechless.

"He doesn't believe us!" Ned said, his freckles were standing out on his pale face, so Nanny knew he was as shocked as she was. "Why doesn't he believe us?"

"I don't know," answered Nanny. "I'm going to blow my whistle for King Brian."

With that, Nanny blew hard on her whistle, but no noise came from it. "What's wrong with this thing?" asked Nanny "It didn't make any noise."

"I'll blow my whistle," said Ned "Maybe yours is broken." Ned pulled his from his pocket and blew it as hard as he could. No noise came from it. "What's wrong with mine?" pouted Ned. "It doesn't work!"

"I'll blow mine," said Henry Daly. He lowered his head to grab the whistle hanging from his collar and blew as hard as he could. Not a sound came from his whistle either.

CHAPTER THIRTEEN

"What's wrong with our whistles?" asked Nanny with her hand on her hip, "I hope King Brian didn't trick us again."

"Indeed I didn't trick you," a voice said. "My ears are still ringing out of my skull you blew those whistles so hard."

It was King Brian. He was sitting on the branch of the tree above their heads with his hands over his ears. "Your pipes are working loud and clear," he said.

"King Brian!" yelled Nanny, Ned and Henry Daly together. They were delighted to see him. Bertie and Frosty neighed in unison, they tossed their heads and pawed the ground. They too were happy to see King Brian.

"Sure we thought the whistles were broken because we couldn't hear the sound of them," said Ned.

"The Leprechaun Kings are the only ones who can hear them," answered King Brian, "and I wouldn't be a bit surprised if every leprechaun King in Ireland showed up. I'm sure their ears are in the same state as mine, but I'll forgive you this time," he laughed. "What can I do for Nanny Reilly, Ned Franey and Henry Daly today?"

"King Brian," said Nanny, "We told Fran O'Toole you gave us Bertie and Frosty and he told us to go home because he had no time for jokes, he had to save Mike Donovan from the Banshee.

"The Banshee?" replied King Brian. "Save Mike Donovan?"

King Brian jumped from the branch to the ground, looking as if he were flying. "It sounds to me like someone is in trouble," he said as he landed. Maybe even on the way to the Banshee's Cradle. Tell me what happened from the very beginning."

Nanny, Ned and Henry Daly told King Brian all about the footprints in the sand. How they and followed them deep into the forest and found an exhausted Fran O'Toole.

"We told Fran O'Toole you could help him find his friend Mike Donovan," said Ned removing his cowboy hat and scratching his head in confusion.

"Then he asked us who King Brian was," interrupted Nanny, "and we said you were king of the leprechauns of Coolrainy." Nanny was so disappointed. She was finding it hard to believe that Fran O'Toole was mad at them, and had rejected their offer of King Brian's help when he really needed it.

"Well now lass," said King Brian shrugging his soldiers in the same disbelief as Nanny and Ned. "Not everybody believes in leprechauns."

"What will we do about Fran O'Toole?" asked Ned.

"We may forget about Fran O'Toole for now," said King Brian. "We need to find the Banshee's Cradle and save Mike Donovan, and we don't have much time."

"We need to find the Banshee's Cradle!" said Nanny, her voice beginning to tremble.

Ned's face turned white, even his freckles paled, he tried to speak but he couldn't.

"Aye lass, I'm sorry to say this," answered King Brian, "but we're the only ones who can save Mike Donovan now."

Nanny and Ned reluctantly agreed. Henry Daly was anxious to get started.

"I'm ready to go," said Henry Daly.

"I suppose we are too then," answered Nanny. She acknowledged a simple Nod from Ned as he took a deep breath.

"I suppose we are," he said.

"King Brian, Fran O'Toole told us to get up on our magic ponies. Are our ponies magic?" Nanny asked.

"Only if you want them to be magic ponies," replied King Brian with a twinkle in his eye. He reached into his cloak and took out a little green notebook. He flicked through the pages and stopped at one.

"Let me see now, in my book, Nanny Reilly, Ned Franey and Henry Daly each have a gold whistle, and anyone who has a leprechaun's gold whistle is as magic as a leprechaun himself." He looked up from the notebook. "Or herself, as the case may be."

"May I wish for Frosty to be a magic pony then?" Nanny asked.

"And may I wish for Bertie to be a magic pony too? added Ned.

"You may," King Brian said, he knew both Nanny and Ned were not aware of the magic power they really had. It was going to take a little getting used to. He put his little green notebook back in his cloak pocket, folded his arms giving them the opportunity to realize their newfound powers. "You may wish for whatever you like, and you don't need me to grant your wishes. You can grant them to yourselves with a snap of your fingers"

Nanny and Ned glanced at each other. Nanny made sure her stampede cord was tight. Ned put his cowboy hat back on and tightened his stampede cord.

"Wish with me Ned," Nanny said as she reached for Ned's hand. "Let's say our wish together."

Nanny Reilly and Ned Franey shut their eyes as tight as they could and said in unison, "I wish Bertie and Frosty were magic ponies." For a moment after their wish, they continued to keep their eyes closed. They both had a firm grip on each other's hand.

"It's alright," chuckled King Brian, you can open your eyes now.

They opened their eyes and looked over at Bertie and Frosty. Both ponies had returned to grazing the long grass again.

"They don't look any different," said Nanny doubting both her and Ned's magic powers.

"Is Bertie a magic pony now?" asked Ned when he opened his eyes.

"He surely is," answered King Brian smiling.

"And is Frosty a magic pony too?" asked Nanny.

"Indeed she is Lass," said King Brian. "Now Bertie and Frosty are magic ponies just like the leprechaun ponies. They can jump over anything and run faster than the wind."

"Can Bertie and Frosty fly?" asked Ned.

"They surely can," answered King Brian. "They can fly over the moon if you ask them to."

"I want to be magic, too!" said Henry Daly. "I wish I was a magic dog who can fly."

"And indeed you shall fly Henry Daly," answered King Brian. Even though Henry had just given himself flying powers by his words, King Brian wanted to show off and demonstrate the grandiose way of granting wishes. He reached into his cloak one more time and took out his shillelagh. He placed it in front of Henry Daly's nose and waved it like a magic wand. Henry stood to attention as King Brian said the words,

"May Henry Daly's wish come true,
May he fly o'er the ocean blue.
May his good nose be keen and able,
To fly us to the Banshee's Cradle."

Henry felt magical. He stood himself taller and stuck his chest out. At that very moment he knew he could fly.

"Are we all magic now King Brian?" asked Nanny Reilly.

"Every last one of us Lass," answered King Brian, "but we must hurry, we haven't a moment to loose.

"Up on your ponies now, Nanny Reilly and Ned Franey, and hold on tight," King Brian put his shillelagh back in his cloak. He bent his legs at the knees and sprang himself up on Henry' back. "This is where the real magic begins."

Nanny and Ned quickly untied Bertie and Frosty and jumped on their backs.

"Are you scared Nanny?" asked Ned.

"Yes, I am Ned," replied Nanny, "but who's going to save Mike Donovan if we don't." They both checked their stampede cords and took a deep breath.

King Brian yelled out, "Up up, and away, Henry Daly! Take me to the Banshee's Cradle!"

Nanny shouted, "Up up, and away, Frosty! Take me to the Banshee's Cradle!"

"Up up, and away, Bertie!" Yelled Ned. "Take me to the Banshee's Cradle!"

CHAPTER FOURTEEN

Henry Daly with King Brian on his back led the way to the Banshee's Cradle. Nanny and Ned held on to Bertie and Frosty for dear life as they left the forest behind them. Their ponies leaped forward and cantered up in the air. The tall pines below got smaller and smaller. They soared high in the sky and they could see the entire coastline, the forestry, and their village, Coolrainy. Nanny and Ned's eyes and mouth were wide open with delight. This was more exhilarating than the chair-o-plane ride at the carnival. Bertie and Frosty's manes and tails blew in the wind, as did King Brian's cloak. Henry Daly's mouth was slightly open with a big bright smile on his face. Soon the coastline and their village faded in the background as they made their descent into the heart of the forest.

Henry and the ponies landed near the entrance of the Banshee's Cradle. They took in the scene before them. Nanny trembled her eyes widening and her knees weakening. Heavy gray clouds darkened the sky. A tall wall made of skulls draped in cobwebs stared back at them. The main gates were made of thighbones. Through the gates, they could see a path that wound its way through dead trees. Cobwebs were everywhere. At the gate sat two skeletons playing cards. They were dressed in old torn uniforms and referring to each other as 'skeleguard.' They argued about who had won the pot, which was a jumble of old teeth. At the skeleguards' feet, two angry looking black dogs wearing spiked collars gnawed on large, blood-covered bones.

Nanny was frightened, and she bet Ned was, too. She and Ned had a daunting task ahead of them, rescuing Mike Donovan from the

Banshee's Cradle. She wasn't sure that even they, the bravest children in Ireland, were equal to it. They needed to get past the skeleguards at the gate and Nanny Reilly knew just how to do that. She didn't have a shillelagh, but she could snap her fingers.

"May the attention be on the bones and cards,
and may we walk past these skeleguards.
May the gates swing open and let us through,
and may we find our very next clue."

Nanny snapped her fingers, and sure enough the bony gates slowly squeaked their way open.

"Good Lass Nanny Reilly," smiled King Brian, "you have it now.

Nanny and Ned looked at each other. They didn't say anything. But their facial expressions said it all. They really were magic.

"Let's go, my friends," chuckled King Brian, The Banshee's Cradle awaits."

They walked through the main gates without the skeleguards even looking in their direction. The skeleguards continued to play their card game and argue. The dogs never took their eyes or their teeth off their bones.

The winding pathway took them to a crossroads where a signpost made of bones stood. The sign pointing to the east said, "New Arrivals," the sign to the west said, "Departures," and the sign to the north said, "Dreary Castle."

"Which way will we go?" Nanny asked. At that, the New Arrivals sign fell off the signpost and pointed to the east.

"It seems to me," said King Brian laughing, "that sign is our very next clue and surely telling us which direction Mike Donovan is. This is the way, my friends. We're getting closer."

"Look!" Ned said, pointing at the sky. Overhead, the biggest crows any of them had ever seen held ropes made from braided hair in their beaks. Dangling at the end of the ropes, was a big wooden cage with someone inside it.

"That's Fran O'Toole in the cage!" cried Nanny. "The Banshee caught him too."

"Saints preserve us," said King Brian. "We'll have to follow that crow before he gets out of sight. If not, it could be too late for Fran O'Toole as well as Mike Donovan.

Hold on tight everybody, we're going up again. "Up up, and away Henry Daly," cried King Brian.

"Up up, and away Frosty," yelled Nanny.

"Up up, and away Bertie," Ned shouted.

They flew into the dark cloudy sky, and followed the crows that were taking Fran O'Toole to New Arrivals. As they flew, they saw more crows carrying wooden cages by braided hair ropes.

"There's people in those cages!" cried Ned.

"What are we going to do, King Brian?" asked Nanny.

"Saints preserve the lot of us," King Brian said. "What have we let ourselves in for? Hold on now the pair of you, the crows are about to land."

The crows hovered over an aged steam train with weathered wooden carriages. Each flock of crows dropped their cage into one of the carriages.

Henry Daly and the posse landed behind an old wooden shed. Large letters on the front of the train spelled out SkelOrientation Express. It had a skeleton at the controls dressed in an old torn engineer's uniform.

"All aboard," shouted the skelegineer, as he blew a whistle that was attached to a chain made of teeth which hung from his neck. "Next stop, Skele Resources."

He blew the whistle one more time and the old train slowly started to move. Black smoke puffed its way out of the smokestack. The engines wheels grinded their way along the tracks. Thick clouds of steam emerged from the belly of the train. The whistle blows screeched their way from the train's pipe as the skelegineer pulled down on a cord.

"Hurry, hurry!" said King Brian. "We'll have to catch that train. Get ready to jump on board as it rolls by." The train reached the shed they were hiding behind.

"Now," shouted King Brian. "Jump".

Nanny and Ned held on to their ponies as tight as they could and asked Bertie and Frosty to jump into the empty stock carriage at the end of the old steam train. The ponies in their best flying pose, lifted themselves from the ground, glided through the open doors and gracefully landed inside the carriage. Henry Daly liked what he saw, so he imitated the efforts of Bertie and Frosty, and made a graceful entrance.

They were all on their way to Skele Resources on the SkelOrientation Express.

CHAPTER FIFTEEN

"Fran O'Toole is going to get a big shock when they see us on our magic ponies with our talking dog and King of the leprechauns of Coolrainy," said Ned.

"Indeed he is," chuckled King Brian, "and Mike Donovan too."

"Next time I won't scare the living daylights out of him," said Henry Daly, remembering his first encounter with Fran O'Toole. "I won't growl at him again, I'll just smile and wag my tail.

"He'll surely be happy to see us this time," said Nanny Reilly. "Hold on Fran O'Toole, hold on Mike Donovan. The bravest children in Ireland are on their way to help you."

"And the bravest dog in Ireland," added Henry Daly, with his newfound smile.

"This is the first time I've been on a train," said Ned. Then he paused for a moment. He thought this was a good opportunity for him to practice a little with his magic powers. "Watch what I can do," he said with a grin.

"May the wind be behind us,
May our hearts be filled with laughter,
May the hand of the skelegineer,
Make this train go faster!"

Ned snapped his fingers and the train suddenly picked up speed.

"Let's see if we can stand like statues and not fall over when the train goes around a bend," said Nanny.

"Yeah!" replied Ned, "that'll be fun."

The two jumped down from their ponies and stood firmly on the floor of the carriage with their feet together and their arms tightly tucked into their sides. As the train picked up speed, Nanny and Ned began to loose their footing and bump off each other. The train got faster and faster and they both found it harder to even stand. They finally sat on the floor of the carriage laughing at each other's silly attempts to get up. Bertie and Frosty were a little wide eyed. They both moved their legs a little wider apart to find balance. Henry Daly wanted to play the game and fall over, but it wasn't so easy for him to fall while he was standing on four legs like Bertie and Frosty.

King Brian had a solemn look on his face. His lips were pressed tightly together and the lines on his forehead showed. He sat quietly on Henry's back and watched the antics of Nanny and Ned.

The skelegineer tried everything he could to slow the train down. He pulled on the emergency brake cord over and over again. He tried his best to put the steam train's furnace out by throwing bucket after bucket of water onto the fire. But the train wouldn't slow down. The carriages were almost coming off the tracks.

The skelegineer shouted, "Help! Help! Runaway train! Runaway train! Stay out of the way!"

The train entered a tunnel dimly lit by torches, which were held by bats that hung from the ceiling of the tunnel. The wind produced by the speeding train blew out the torches, and the bats dug their claws into the tunnel walls to avoid being swept along with the train.

When the train finally emerged from the tunnel Nanny, Ned and King Brian heard a clanging sound. It was a railway crossing. The skelegineer had his skelehands over his eyes.

"I don't think the train is going to stop!" said Nanny.

"There's a carriage on the tracks!" added Ned nervously. "We might crash into it."

King Brian had a feeling it would come to this. He raised himself from Henry Daly's back and hovered in mid air. He once again reached into his cloak and retrieved his shillelagh. He held it high in the air and said the words.

"May the wheels stop rolling,

And may the brakes find their lock,
May the SkelOrientation Express
Come to a mighty stop"

The train suddenly came to a stop. The skelegineer's bones rattled in fright.

"That was fun going fast!" said Nanny excitedly. "I've never gone that fast before."

"Me neither!" said Ned, secretly hoping not to go as fast as that again.

King Brian landed gently on the floor of the carriage still wearing his frown. Nanny Reilly sensed he wasn't too happy with herself and Ned for some reason.

"Is everything alright King Brian? Quizzed Nanny, "wasn't that fun?" she added.

"Indeed it wasn't fun," replied King Brian. "Ned used his magic powers in the wrong way and put us all in danger. Answer me this, the pair of you. If I didn't stop the train at the very last moment like I did, when did either one of you plan to stop it?"

Nanny looked at Ned for the answer, and Ned returned Nanny's look.

"If you continue using your magic like that you'll both end up at Ravens Point for playing mean tricks on people with not a friend in the world."

"I'm sorry King Brian," said Ned as he and Nanny bowed their heads in shame. "I just forgot myself. I don't ever want to be mean again."

"Or me either King Brian," added Nanny, "will you help us to be good and use our wishes well?"

"It's all my fault," sighed King Brian. I didn't prepare any of you for the magic powers that you have. We don't have time for a lesson in wishes right now. All I can say is this. Every wish you make has to be for the good of human kind and animal kind. We are not here for fun and games, there will be plenty of time for that. Our mission here is to rescue Fran O'Toole and Mike Donovan from the Banshee's Cradle. If any of us become a victim of the Banshee we will become powerless. So it is vital that we don't get caught," continued King Brian. "Now tighten up your stampede cords and let me see the two bravest children in Ireland put their best foot forward."

Nanny and Ned liked the fact that they were on a mission. They straightened up their shoulders, stood tall and tightened their stampede cords.

Nanny, Ned, King Brian, and Henry Daly all peeked over the side of the carriage and saw two skeleguards on horses riding over the tracks. Long black capes covered the horses from head to hoof. Behind them, two more horses in the same black capes pulled a black carriage. Each carriage door bore a skull with the words 'Dreary Castle Guest Shuttle.'

Nanny, Ned, King Brian and Henry Daly, could see the train station surrounded by old, broken-down wooden buildings. It looked like a ghost town. Two horses dressed in the same long black attire were tied to a hitching post.

The skelegineer was still shook up after his out of control train ride. His bones clattered and his teeth rattled together. Shaking, he blew his whistle again and shouted, "We are now approaching Skele Resources, and all passengers prepare for pick up." He then noisily chattered his way off the train scratching his head with one hand and holding his box of tools with the other.

"Prepare for pick up. What does that mean?" asked Ned.

"We're going to find out right now," King Brian said, as he looked up and saw an oversized crow with a six-foot wingspan hovering above their heads.

"What happened to your cage?" cawed the crow.

King Brian stood up on Henry Daly's head. He looked up at the enormous crow, placed both hands on his hips and said, "I think we got on the wrong train."

"Do you have your tickets?" cawed the crow again.

"We were in such a hurry to catch the train, we were too late to get tickets," King Brian said.

"Do you think we could get tickets now?"

"Only guests of the Banshee get tickets. Are you guests of the Banshee?" asked the crow.

"We surely are," said King Brian. "On midsummer's eve the Banshee invited us here, so here we are." King Brian casually turned to Nanny and Ned and winked at them. Nanny and Ned didn't speak. They nodded profusely.

"What are your names?" cawed the crow suspiciously. "I need to check the guest list."

"We're called The Rescueteers," answered King Brian as he stuck his chest out and held the lapels of his waistcoat. "I'm sure we're on the guest list."

"Wait here and don't move until I come back," said the crow pointing at The Rescueteers with one wing. He then flew away.

"Let's get out of here as quickly as we can," said King Brian. 'We only have minute or two."

Nanny and Ned made sure their stampede cords were tight and they jumped up on their ponies. Frosty began pawing the floor of the carriage. She felt the anxiety, and was just as anxious to get off the train as Nanny and Ned were. Bertie was also getting restless. Henry Daly knew he had to step up to the plate and get everyone to safety.

CHAPTER SIXTEEN

Henry peered out the carriage door and quickly scanned the old buildings before him. One old building in particular had a lower profile than the others. It sat further back and at a glance was hard to notice. "Follow me!" said Henry Daly. "There's an old wooden building over here."

Nanny, Ned and King Brian were quietly relieved as Henry quickly and confidently leaped from the train with King Brian still on board. Bertie and Frosty were only too happy to follow Henry wherever he may lead them. They sprang from the carriage. Nanny and Ned held on tight. They were remembering King Brian's words just after the scolding he gave them.

"If any of us become a victim of the Banshee we will become powerless". He said. "So it is vital we don't get caught."

Nanny could feel her heart pound. This was the most afraid she had ever felt, but it was too late to turn back now. Ned's thoughts and feelings were exactly like Nanny's. But they had to put their fears to one side and remember why they were there. They were the two bravest children in Ireland, on a mission to save Fran O'Toole and Mike Donovan.

The old building covered in cobwebs had two doors. Above one door was written: "Skeletees Only," and above the other door: "Skeledeliveries Only." The Rescueteers scurried through the Skeletees Only door, and shut it behind them.

"That was a close one," said Nanny. "That big old crow sure was scary. What are we going to do now, King Brian?"

"We'll have to stay out of sight," answered King Brian. "As soon as the Banshee hears about The Rescueteers, she's going to be looking for us. We'll have to be very careful."

No sooner had those words come out of King Brian's mouth, when they heard horns going off.

"What's that noise?" asked Ned.

"It sounds like an alarm signal," answered King Brian. "They've discovered we're missing. Now they are going to search everywhere for us."

Inside the old building a corridor led to two doors. "Skeliforms" was printed on the door on the right, and the door on the left said "Skelekitchen." They heard the clatter of marching skeleguards outside the Skeletee's Only door. King Brian reached for his shillelagh and waved in small precise circles. He focused on the Skeliforms door and said the words,

"May the Skeliform door open wide,
May we be on the other side.
The Rescueteers have been called to rise,
So may we find a fine disguise."

The Skeliform door opened wide.

"Quickly, in here," said King Brian. Henry Daly briskly trotted through the open door with King Brian on his back. Bertie and Frosty were still close at Henry's heels with Nanny and Ned still clinging tight.

Inside they found uniforms of all different types, and all were old and torn. There were hundreds of them in rows, hanging as they would in a dry cleaners store.

They wandered among the rows of skeliforms.

"Look!" said Henry Daly. "Here are some of those spiked dog collars."

"And those look like the skeliform the train driver was wearing," added Nanny Reilly.

Henry Daly sniffed his way through the rows of skeliforms. "They all smell like the old bones I have buried in the back yard," he thought to himself. "No wonder they are all torn to shreds. I bet those two guard dogs got their teeth stuck into them and tore them up."

King Brian scanned the rows of old torn clothes looking for the perfect disguise. "Hold it right there Henry Daly," he said. I believe we have found the answer. He pointed his shillelagh at the hanging skeliforms. He removed two from the rack and floated them towards Nanny and Ned.

"I want the pair of you to put these on," he said. "From here on you need to be skelecooks." Nanny and Ned dismounted from their ponies and put on the old torn cook's uniform, but they were much too big. The sleeves hung down to the ground. The pants were so big that Nanny Reilly's whole body fit in one leg. If Ned got into the other leg, there would still be plenty of room left for Henry Daly.

"These skeliforms are too big, King Brian," said Ned disappointedly

"King Brian," said Nanny, "If I said the magic words to make them fit us, would that be for the good of human kind?" Nanny wanted to be sure she was using her magic powers for all the right reasons. Another scolding from King Brian was not what she wanted to hear. What if she ended up in Ravens Point with not a friend in the world? Not only that, what if she ended up with rabbit's ears and a pig's nose? Topped off with a mushroom! Nanny shuddered at the thought.

"It surely would be for the good of human kind Nanny Reilly," answered King Brian. "It would be for the good of Fran O'Toole, Mike Donovan, and ourselves." The King put his shillelagh back in his cloak pocket. He leaned back and folded his arms giving Nanny the floor.

Nanny glared at the skeliforms and said the words,

"May these skeliforms shrink,
And fit just right,
And may they be
Our disguise tonight!"

Then she snapped her fingers. Suddenly Nanny and Ned's skeliforms began shrinking until they fit perfectly. "Now we're cooks!" said Nanny with excitement.

"Do cooks wear cowboy hats?" asked Ned not wanting to remove his hat.

"They do indeed," replied King Brian, "but they wear tall cowboy hats with no lid, so a leprechaun King like myself can stand on top of a Rescueteer's head and look out over the top."

"Well then, King Brian," said Ned understanding his role as a Rescueteer, "may I say the magic words for the good of human kind and make our cowboy hats tall cook's cowboy hats."

"Yes you may," said King Brian. He knew at that very moment that Nanny and Ned would carry the torch and represent leprechaun magic well at all times, wherever they go.

Ned took a deep breath and said the magic words,

"May our hats grow tall,
And look just fine,
May there be plenty of room
To hide King Brian."

Then Ned snapped his fingers, and sure enough the crown of their cowboy hats grew to ten inches tall. Now King Brian could stand on his toes and peep out whenever necessary.

Nanny and Ned smiled at each other as they admired their unusually tall cowboy hats.

"What about me?" asked Henry Daly. "What will I be?"

"You could disguise yourself as a guard dog Henry Daly," said King Brian. "Wear one of those spiked collars."

"I'll put it on you, Henry Daly," Nanny said reaching for one of the collars.

"What will Bertie and Frosty disguise themselves as?" asked Ned. "None of these skeliforms will fit them."

"Look around for black capes like the ones the skeleguards horses were wearing," said King Brian. "There must be some here somewhere."

"I found them!" Ned said. "Here they are." Ned stood beside a large wooden crate with "Skelecarriage Horses" written on it. He lifted the lid. Inside he found black capes like the Banshee's horses wore. They put the capes on Bertie and Frosty, but they too were much too big. Bertie and Frosty looked like clothes hangers for the capes.

"King Brian, what about leprechaun magic for the good of animal kind," asked Henry Daly as he studied Bertie and Frosty's oversized garments. He wanted to help them out and make them look good in their carriage horse capes.

"Leprechaun magic for the good of animal kind is a good thing Henry Daly," answered King Brian. "Are you going to help Bertie and Frosty out with alterations to their attire."

"I certainly am," replied Henry Daly. Henry took a step back and sized up Bertie and Frosty. He raised his right paw and pointed it at the ponies. He spoke the magic words,

"May Bertie and Frosty's
Capes size down.
May they be the best dressed
Ponies in town."

And sure enough, the capes started to shrink until they fit Bertie and Frosty perfectly.

"Now they look like real carriage horses," said Ned. "The skeleguards will never recognize them."

"I'm the wrong color dog," said Henry Daly, realizing he needed to change his own appearance before they made their way amongst the Banshee's skeletees. "I'm a brindle dog. The skeleguard's dogs are black. They might recognize me and catch me. I wonder what will they do to me if they catch me?"

"They might take you over to Departures," said Ned.

"I won't let them catch you, Henry Daly," said Nanny Reilly. "Don't worry. I'll say the magic words for your disguise. Nanny focused her eyes on Henry Daly, and said the magic words,."

"May Henry Daly
Be no longer brindle,
May he turn black
So he can mingle."

Another click of Nanny's fingers and Henry Daly, the last of The Rescueteers, was now in disguise and ready to aid in the rescue mission of Fran O'Toole and Mike Donovan.

Now all The Rescueteers had their disguises. King Brian elevated himself from Henry Daly's back and landed on top of Nanny's head. Her tall chef's cowboy hat hid him well.

"It's time we made ourselves worthy of our name," said King Brian. "Is everybody ready. He held his shillelagh high in the air. "Onward leprechaun soldiers, duty calls. Help is on the way Fran O'Toole and Mike Donovan.

Nanny and Ned tightened their stampede cords. The Rescueteers left the old wooden building. Henry Daly led the way. All around them, skeleguards were combing the area, searching for the intruders.

The skeleguards horses stood at a weathered hitching post, guarded by a large black crow.

"We can tie Bertie and Frosty up over there," said Nanny pointing to the hitching post.

"What about that crow?" asked Ned.

"Don't worry about the crow," said King Brian, looking out over the top of Nanny's cowgirl chef's hat. "You're in disguise now. That crow has no idea who you are."

"That's true," said Ned, suddenly realizing that he was now a skelecook. "We can just walk over there and tie up Bertie and Frosty, and that crow won't know who we are." Nanny and Ned nervously walked the ponies to the hitching post with Henry Daly between them. They began to tie up Bertie and Frosty.

"Hold it right there," cawed the crow, his wings spread wide.

Nanny and Ned started to shake. The hair on Henry Daly's back stood upright. King Brian kept himself out of sight as he crouched down in Nanny's hat.

"There's no free parking here," cawed the crow. "If you're going to tie those ponies up to my hitching post, it's going to cost you two pairs of teeth. One pair for each pony."

"I don't have two pairs of teeth," said Nanny Reilly disappointedly. Nanny was afraid to use her magic powers in front of the crow. She didn't want him to hear her use any magic words. He would start cawing and screeching for the skeleguards. Then they'd be brought to the Banshee and loose all their powers.

"How could you not have two pairs of teeth?" snapped the crow. "Today is payday. We just got paid twenty minutes ago. You should have at least two pairs of teeth in your pocket."

Ned came to Nanny's rescue. "They fell out through the holes in our skelichef pants. May we owe you two pairs of teeth?" he asked politely.

"Owe me two pairs of teeth!" yelled the crow, as he stood taller on the hitching post and spread his wings as high and wide as he could. This is the Banshee's Cradle we're in, nobody gets any favors here!" The crow squinted. His black beady eyes peered into Ned's eyes. He side stepped along the hitching post, leaned forward and squinted at Nanny. "What are your names?" he asked, "I'm going to report the two of you to the skeleguards for vagrancy. You don't even have two pairs of teeth between the pair of you."

Nanny trembled,' she was close to tears. "I wish I did," she replied with a quiver in her voice.

"Done," whispered King Brian. Two pairs of teeth appeared in Nanny's hands.

"This is no place for comedians," cawed the crow grabbing the teeth from Nanny. "You're lucky to get parking. The Banshee's banquet is tonight. Every hitching post will soon be full. And don't think I'm going to let you have free parking when your time is up. You have one skelihour, then I want more teeth. Remember that!"

"He's a mean crow, King Brian" Nanny whispered as she, Ned, and Henry Daly walked away. "I wish he wasn't so mean."

As soon as Nanny Reilly said those words, the crow called them back. "I'm feeling so happy today," he said, "I want to give you your teeth back. Park here as long as you like." Then he cawed as loudly as he could, "Free parking all day and night for everyone!"

Skeleguards who had their horses hitched at another hitching post, untied them and hustled to the free parking spot. They tied their horses and walked away; laughing and putting the teeth they saved back in their skeliform pockets.

"I'll stay out here with Bertie and Frosty and keep watch," said Henry Daly.

"Good idea, Henry Daly," whispered a voice from inside Nanny's hat. "We don't want those two fine magic ponies falling into the wrong hands."

"Be careful, Henry Daly," Nanny Reilly said quietly. "Shout as loud as you can if you need our help. We'll be back as soon as we find Fran O'Toole."

Ned and Nanny Reilly headed off toward Skele Resources at the other side of the train station. King Brian balanced himself on Nanny's head as she walked. Skeleguards were combing the buildings, looking for two children, one black pony, one white pony, a tiny man wearing a crown and a black and brown dog.

CHAPTER SEVENTEEN

At Skele Resources, Fran O'Toole was waiting in a long line for his turn. The Rescueteers joined the end of the line. A skeleguard with a guard dog kept watch over the line of new arrivals. There was a skeleton wearing an old torn two-piece gray suit and was sitting at an old coffin. She was called a skelesource. In her skelehand she had a finger bone with a long fingernail. It was her pen. She was dipping the fingernail into black ink and writing on dried rabbit hides. She had a stack of hides on her coffin desk. On her desk, were two trays. One was labeled: "Awaiting Possibilities," and the other read: "Future Possibilities."

"Next," said the skelesource in a loud, scratchy voice. The skeleguard pushed Fran O'Toole forward.

"Move along," he told Fran angrily.

Fran turned to the skeleguard and yelled, "I'm tired being pushed around by you. Why don't you just take me to Departures and get it over with?"

"You'll get there soon enough," snarled the skeleguard angrily. "Now move it. You're holding everything up. All new arrivals have to be checked in. Get going." He pushed Fran O'Toole again.

"Name?" asked the skelesource. She didn't even look up.

"Fran O'Toole," answered Fran. The skelesource dipped her finger pen into the black ink and wrote Fran's name on a dried out rabbit hide.

"Address?" asked the Skelesource.

"Culleton's Gap, Ireland," Fran answered reluctantly.

"Do you have any living relatives?" she asked, still not looking up.

"Yes," Fran answered.

"Are any of them sick, dying, or in the hospital?" asked the skelesource.

"I've a brother in the hospital," said Fran.

"What's his name?"

"Why do you want to know?" shouted Fran.

"What's his name?" snarled the skelesource again. The skeleguard pushed Fran one more time.

"Sean O'Toole," replied Fran sadly.

"What hospital is he in?" asked the Skelesource.

"That's none of your business," Fran yelled.

"Answer her," the skeleguard growled as he pushed Fran again. "Everybody sick, dying, or in the hospital is our business."

"What hospital is he in?" the skelesource asked again as though nothing had happened.

"He's in the County Hospital," said Fran, "but he's not dying. He just has a concussion."

"If he's in hospital, he's still a possibility," the skelesource said. "What ward is he in?"

Fran held his head low. "Ward 101," he said sadly.

The skelesource wrote the information on another dried out hide. She rolled it up like a scroll. Tied it with a piece of braided hair, and put it in the "Awaiting Possibilities" tray.

"How many other living relatives do you have?" she asked.

"Nine," Fran answered with his head still held low.

"Do they reside at the same address?" asked the skelesource.

"Yes," answered Fran softly.

The skelesource wrote Frans' relatives information on another hide, and rolled it up into a scroll. She tied it with another piece of braided hair and put it in the "Future Possibilities" tray. Then she rolled up the hide with Fran's information on it and handed it to him. "Take this with you through that door and wait to be called," she said pointing to a large wooden door with a skull painted on it. She then shouted, "Next!"

Hanging from the top of the skull painted door holding a box made of big toe bones, was a large bat. He resembled a rat with leather wings.

"Empty your pockets into this," said the bat in a hoarse high-pitched voice. Fran O'Toole emptied his pockets into the big toe bone box and disappeared behind the door.

Nanny, Ned and King Brian had caught up with Fran O'Toole, and were a few 'New Arrivals' behind him in line. They heard every question the Skelesource asked him.

"Did you hear all that?" said Nanny Reilly.

"Indeed I did," answered King Brian.

"Is that skelesource going to ask us the same questions?" asked Ned.

"I wish this line of people would go home," said Nanny Reilly. "Then it would be our turn, and we'd be right behind Fran O'Toole."

Suddenly the line of people disappeared, and The Rescueteers were next in line.

The skeleguard was running up and down, pulling his dog in every direction. He ran in circles, scratching his head. The guard dog, dizzy from all the running around, fell over. Nanny and Ned stood in front of the skelesource shaking. King Brian kept out of sight.

"Name," she said not even looking up.

Before anyone could answer, a loud deep voice from nowhere yelled, "What are you two doing here?"

Nanny Reilly and Ned turned around; they saw a tall wide skelechef. He was the head skelechef.

"Do you know this is one of the busiest nights of the year, and we are already short-handed. Don't give me any excuses. I don't want to hear them. Get yourselves into the skelekitchen and start preparing those lizard livers."

The two new skelecooks high-tailed it to the skelekitchen without saying a word.

"That was a close one," said Ned.

"I thought we were goners," Nanny Reilly said. "He was one angry skelechef."

"King Brian, do you know how to prepare lizard livers?" Ned asked.

"I surely don't. My specialty is corned beef and cabbage with plenty of new spuds, a good dose of farmers butter and a big mug of buttermilk," King Brian said proudly as he patted his well-rounded tummy and smacked his lips together.

The head skelechef marched over to Nanny and Ned with a large tub of lizard livers. "You've one skelihour to get these ready for the Banshee's Banquet tonight. Get cracking. I've other things to do," the skelechef shouted at Nanny and Ned.

The two looked around and saw the other skelecooks were rushing around the skelekitchen and preparing other things. One skelecook was tucked into a corner plucking chickens. Feathers were floating all around him but he didn't seem to notice. He threw the plucked birds into roasting pans with the heads and feet still attached. Another skelecook was shaking seasonings over trays of fish heads and yelling at his helper to get them in the oven before the chicken. Several baskets of seaweed were stacked on top of each other on a butcher's block. Two skelecooks were chopping the seaweed to smithereens with meat cleavers and then throwing it into a large pot.

In the heart of the skelekitchen, the head skelechef and three other skelechefs fussed over a four tier, what seemed to be, cake. It was all black with snails all around the base of it and a figurine of a Banshee on the top tier proudly holding a skull.

Other skelecooks were moving quickly around the kitchen carrying trays of food from the ovens to the worktops, from the worktops to the stoves. Nobody even noticed Nanny and Ned.

"We've no one to show us how to make these lizard livers." Ned said, "Everyone is busy.

"Don't worry, Ned," Nanny Reilly said as she rolled her sleeves up. "I think I know how to make them."

Nanny and Ned were two short to reach the stove, so they placed two pots upside down on the floor in front of the stove, and stood on them.

"I think we should boil the lizard livers," said Nanny. My mother boils everything, except on Sundays when she roasts a chicken. What do you think Ned?"

"I think you're right Nanny," answered Ned. He wasn't sure how his mother prepared anything. With Ned's help, Nanny poured the lizard livers into a pot on the stove. She studied the containers of various spices on the shelf in front of her. "I never heard of any of these," said Nanny as she held the jar in front of her.

"Ground cartilage. What's that?"

"I don't know," said Ned, "sure can't we put it in anyway?"

Nanny smelled the powder. "Oh yuck," she said as she curled up her nose and held it as far away from herself as she could. "The Banshee is not going to like this." Nanny shook what she thought was an appropriate amount into the lizard livers. She put the lid back on it and placed it back on the shelf.

"I wonder what this smells like," said Ned. He opened a jar of dried crushed veins. Ned didn't have to put the jar to his nose; the odor drifted its way into his nasal cavity causing Ned's eyes to water and his nose to crinkle. Ned couldn't talk. He held his nose with one hand and handed Nanny the jar with the other.

Nanny reached for the jar and kept it as far away from herself as she could. Once again she shook what she thought was an appropriate amount into the lizard livers. Nanny noticed one container larger than all the rest.

"What's written on that big one in the corner," she asked Ned. "Can you reach it?"

Ned leaned forward and reached for the container. He held in front of him and read what was written in large bold letters: "Warning! Dizzy Dust. For Departures Only!"

King Brian peeped over the top of Nanny's hat. "I think that's one ingredient you should put in to your concoction," he said.

Ned passed Nanny the container. She opened it and shook several ounces in.

"Ah sure, put a little bit more in," smiled King Brian, "don't be shy."

"How much more?" Nanny asked

"Every ounce of it," answered King Brian. He rubbed his hands together grinning to himself. He felt so triumphant he wanted to kick up his heels, but instead he slapped his leg and wriggled his body.

Nanny emptied the entire container of dizzy dust into the pot. Using a wooden stick with a skeleton's hand attached to the end of it, she stirred all the ingredients together. "This is all stuck together," said Nanny. "I need something to make it stir. Pass me that water over there."

Ned passed two gallons of water to Nanny Reilly. He poured one in and Nanny poured the other. The ingredients loosened up and the lizard livers began to bubble and cook.

"You're a grand cook Nanny Reilly," said King Brian, as he pinched his nostrils shut after inhaling the terrible aroma.

"My mother said the way to a man's heart is through his stomach," said Ned.

"If a woman wants a husband, all she has to do is cook a good dinner with plenty of meat and potatoes in it. Then she'll be walking down the aisle in no time."

"Not if she cooks him something like this," said Nanny, "My dad's greyhounds wouldn't even eat this."

"Nor would O'Brien's pigs," added Ned as he thought about what other animal wouldn't eat it, "and they eat whatever you put in front of them,"

The background noises in the skelekitchen got louder. Skelestewards brought in crockery in preparation for dishing up the various dishes. The Banshee's Banquet was close to getting underway.

"King Brian, how are we going to save Fran O'Toole?" Nanny Reilly asked.

"We'll have to go through the same door he went through and find him," answered King Brian. "When the head skelechef has his back turned, we'll sneak out. Keep stirring those lizard livers Nanny Reilly."

The head skelechef was peering at Nanny and Ned. They took turns stirring the lizard livers until the he turned his back again.

"He's not looking now," said Ned.

"Now is the time then," King Brian said. "Let's get out of here as quick as we can, before he turns around again."

Nanny and Ned left the lizard livers cooking on the stove and crept out of the skelekitchen. They made their way back to Henry Daly and their two magic ponies.

"It's about time," said Henry Daly. "The Dreary Castle guest shuttle has been busy all evening, going back and forth from the train station. The skeleguards are all over the place, and I just saw Fran O'Toole."

"Where is he?" asked Ned.

"He's over there in that wooden cage," said Henry Daly, pointing toward the train station.

"It looks like they are getting ready to take him to Departures," said King Brian.

"Why is he wearing one of those skeliforms?" asked Nanny Reilly. Fran O'Toole was wearing one of the old, torn skeliforms they had seen in the skeliform room.

"Look," said Ned, "there's something written on the cage."

An old piece of wood was haphazardly nailed to the cage. It had a skull painted on it, and the words: "Skeletrustee's Only."

A flock of crows swooped down, took the cage's braided hair ropes in their beaks and hoisted Fran up and over their heads. The crow headed off in the direction of Dreary Castle.

"Quickly everyone," King Brian said as he jumped out from under Nanny Reilly's chef's hat onto Henry Daly's back. "We can't let Fran O'Toole out of our sight. Jump on your magic ponies and hold on tight. Let's get going." Nanny and Ned jumped up on Bertie and Frosty, and prepared for take off.

"Up up, and away, Henry Daly!" King Brian shouted.

"Up up, and away, Frosty!" Nanny Reilly yelled.

"Up up, and away, Bertie!" Ned yelled.

Still safe in their disguises, The Rescuteers took off after Fran O'Toole.

CHAPTER EIGHTEEN

The Rescueteers followed the crows carrying Fran O'Toole to Dreary Castle. The crows dropped Fran's cage at the skeleguards' hut. The Rescueteers landed behind the hut. They could see Dreary Castle. The castle walls were made of skulls and covered in cobwebs. They were just like the walls that surrounded the Banshee's Cradle. Outside the castle's main entrance, awaiting their turn, was a line of horse drawn carriages. Every carriage had two horses covered from head to toe in black capes. About one hundred skeleguards were lined up and standing to attention. The chief skeleguard walked up and down in front of them, tapping his leg with an old spine bone. "Skeleguards," he said, "as you all know, tonight, we have the Banshee's Banquet. Every Banshee in Ireland is here. We must be at our very best. We have to maintain the high standards we are known for throughout the Banshees' industry.

"Tonight, due to a breach in security, every Banshee will have her own personal skeleguard. A group called 'The Rescuteers' was spotted in the Banshee's Cradle earlier. We are not sure if they are still here because we have had not seen them since. We must assume that they are still here. Therefore, it is our duty to protect every Banshee who is here in the Cradle attending the Banshees' Banquet tonight."

"Did you hear all that, King Brian?" Nanny Reilly asked. "They were talking about us!

"Indeed I did hear it," King Brian answered.

"If they catch us, we're surely goners!" Ned said.

One of the skeleguards escorted Fran O'Toole to the side of the castle and took him through an old wooden door marked: "Skeletees Only."

King Brian said, "We need to follow Fran O'Toole through that door and get him out of there as quickly as possible."

"I'll stay here on guard with Bertie and Frosty," said Henry Daly. "We'll be ready to take off when you come out."

"That's a very good idea, Henry Daly," said King Brian. "All right then, Nanny Reilly and Ned Franey, are you ready?"

"We're ready," they answered together, straightening their chef's hats. King Brian returned to his hiding place in Nanny's hat, and they followed Fran O'Toole through the 'Skeletees Only' door. Inside skelewaiters were running about in different directions. Dishes made from skulls were piled up in stacks near an old bathtub.

"There's Fran O'Toole!" Ned said. "He's washing those skull dishes in that old tub."

"The luck of the Irish is with us tonight," King Brian said with a big smile. "Let's grab him and go."

"There you are!" shouted a familiar voice. "I've been looking everywhere for you two!"

Nanny and Ned froze. The head skelechef walked up behind the two of them and ushered them through the skelewaiters, and into the Grand Skeletal Ballroom.

He led them to a platform at the front of the ballroom. Nanny and Ned looked around the room. Before them stood coffins mounted on skeletal feet, and every coffin was draped with a fine layer of cobwebs. At the middle of each coffin, sat a bat on a skull holding a flaming torch. Around these coffins, sat one hundred Banshees. Fifty on each side of the room. They were all dressed in similar black attire. From what Nanny and Ned could see, all the Banshees had wart infested noses, and none of them had any teeth. Behind each Banshee stood a skeleguard.

"Banshees of Ireland," said the head skelechef, as he walked out on center stage. "Tonight, I have received great compliments for the lizard livers. The compliments do not go to the head skelechef this time, they go to the best skelecooks the Banshee's Cradle has ever known. It gives me great pleasure to introduce them to you."

The skelechef took four paces back and left Nanny Reilly and Ned at center stage. The Banshees nodded and howled in approval. The skelechef stepped down from the platform and walked over to the Banshee sitting in the first skelechair to the right. As he pulled out her skelechair, the Banshee rose wobbling a little.

Then she staggered toward Nanny Reilly and Ned Franey on the platform.

"What will we do, King Brian?" Nanny whispered nervously.

Under her hat, King Brian was on his knees clutching rosary beads, his eyes shut tight. "Pray," he whispered, "As hard as you can."

"It gives me great pleasure," the Banshee weaved back and forth, "to have skelecooks like the two of you on the Banshee's Cradle team." She balanced herself against the trophy table. "I have been the General Manager here for one hundred years, and in all those years I have never had lizard livers as good as those I had tonight. She took a deep breath and paused for a moment. The other Banshees howled again. Nanny Reilly and Ned stood like statues.

The Banshee continued. "I have here," she paused again and turned to the right. Reaching out to pick up the skull trophy, she fell backwards towards the skelechef. He caught her, handed her the skull trophy and steadied her. "I have here," she said again. "The highest award any skelecook has ever been given."

Slumped in their skelechairs, the other Banshees howled again. "It is an honor to award this trophy to you both for a job well done," The Banshee was working hard on trying to balance herself as she extended the skull to both Nanny and Ned. The head skelechef gestured to his award winning skelecooks to take the skull trophy. Nervously, Nanny and Ned took short steps toward the Banshee. Nanny Reilly reached out and took the skull.

"Would you like to say a few words," asked the Banshee swaying to and fro. Nanny and Ned shook their heads. The head skelechef took a step toward them.

"Are you sure you wouldn't like to say something?" he asked. "It is a great honor to be awarded the skull trophy."

Nanny and Ned shook their heads again.

"All right," said the skelechef. "I understand your nervousness. It is not easy to speak in front of so many honored guests. You may go back to the skelekitchen now and help the other skelechefs clean up."

Nanny and Ned backed toward the Grand Skeletal Ballroom door, holding the skull trophy. Weaving in their skekechairs, the Banshees howled again. Ned closed the ballroom doors behind them.

"I tried to say thank you, but the words wouldn't come out," said Nanny Reilly, "were you scared, King Brian?" Nanny asked.

No answer came from King Brian.

"King Brian, are you all right?" asked Ned.

"Look into my hat and see if he's still there," said Nanny as she bowed her head low, so Ned could look down into her hat.

"He's still there," said Ned. "He's on his knees with his eyes shut, holding rosary beads. Are you all right, King Brian?"

"Is that you Ned?" King Brian asked.

"Yes, it's me," Ned said.

"Saints preserve us tonight," King Brian said relieved. "I'm proud of the two of you. You stood your ground well."

"That's because we weren't able to talk, King Brian," replied Nanny.

"That Banshee wasn't able to talk or stand to well either," said Ned.

"I think that had something to do with your lizard livers," laughed King Brian.

"Where did Fran O'Toole go?" Nanny asked, looking around.

"All the skull dishes are gone!" said Ned.

"There he is," said King Brian.

Fran O'Toole was being led by a skeleguard.

"Come on. We've got to keep him in our sights," said Nanny Reilly.

The Rescueteers followed closely. The skeleguard marched Fran up a rickety, narrow spiral staircase illuminated by bat torches. The stairs led all the way to the roof of Dreary Castle. On the roof of the castle, there was a skeleguard hut with several wooden cages lined up beside it. Nailed to each cage was an old wooden sign with "Departures" poorly painted on it in black.

Nanny, Ned, and King Brian hid behind the skeleguard hut. Fran was pushed into a cage.

"Your taxi awaits," snarled the laughing skeleguard.

"Fran! Fran!" came a voice from nowhere. Fran turned. There in the wooden cage beside him was his best friend, Mike Donovan!

"Mike!" Fran yelled. "Are you alright?"

"I've been better," answered Mike. "What are we going to do, Fran? We're goners. We need a miracle! Once the Banshee gets hold of you, that's it. There is no tomorrow."

"We'll have to find a way out of here, Mike," said Fran. "Do you have any ideas?"

"No, I don't, Fran," Mike said sadly. "But I'd love to have a last wish right now."

"Maybe I should have listened to those two youngsters I met in the forest," said Fran. "They were talking about getting a wish from a leprechaun."

"What two youngsters? And a wish from what leprechaun?" Mike asked.

"After the Banshee took you away," Fran said, "I followed you all the way into the forest, and then I and fell asleep with exhaustion for a few minutes." Fran told Mike about meeting Nanny Reilly and Ned and how he stormed off on them when they were telling him about some leprechaun king and their talking dog.

"Did they have gold whistles?" asked Mike.

They did," answered Fran. "Even the dog, who they said could talk had a gold whistle. One of the youngsters was about to blow the whistle when I stormed off." Mike started to nod his head in sudden realization. He slowly spoke the words, "Whoever has a leprechaun's gold whistle is as magic as a leprechaun himself." He continued nodding his head

"How do you know that?" asked Fran.

"They were the very words out of my grandfather's mouth to me when I was a young lad," Mike said. "He had a gold whistle. He told his father, my great grandfather, he had gotten it from a leprechaun who called himself, King Brian of Coolrainy because he saved the Kings life. My great grandfather didn't believe him, and took the whistle from him for telling lies".

"King Brian of Coolrainy?" said Fran in astonishment. "That's the leprechaun those two youngsters were talking about."

"You're joking me!" said Mike.

"I'm surely not joking you," replied Fran. "They were closer to me than you are now. I heard them as plain as day say King Brian of Coolrainy, and they were from Coolrainy too!"

"I remember my grandfather telling me not to tell a grownup if I ever met a leprechaun, because not too many of them believe in anything magic. Never were truer words spoken," said Mike. "If those two youngsters tried to tell me about a leprechaun called King Brian and a talking dog, I wouldn't have believed them either."

"Do you think those kids were telling the truth?" Fran asked.

"I would bet my very life, and everything I own on it," answered Mike. "All we can do now is wish for a miracle."

CHAPTER NINETEEN

Fran O'Toole sat in the cage holding his knees into his chest and his head resting on his knees. He felt hopeless. He could do nothing, he could go nowhere, and the worst thing of all was, how sad he felt for not believing Nanny and Ned.

"Mike," he said, "I wish I had believed those youngsters. I know it's too late now, but I wish I could turn back the clock to that very moment in the forest. If I believed in magic I would be home right now, as warm as toast by the fire. Enjoying a good dinner with a bottle of stout and no worries. Instead, here we are, in the Banshee's Cradle of all places. We're locked in wooden cages on the roof of Dreary Castle and about to depart to the place of no return."

"But sure you can't blame yourself Fran," replied Mike, he was trying to console his friend in his final hour. Who's to say I would have done anything differently if the shoe were on the other foot."

A miracle was exactly what they needed.

"What will we do now, King Brian?" asked Nanny.

"We'll have to distract the guard and let Mike Donovan and Fran O'Toole out of those cages," answered King Brian. "Then we'll make a run for it."

"How are we going to distract the guard?" asked Ned.

"We'll tell him, if he hurries, he can get lizard livers in the skelekitchen! Then we'll open the cages and let Fran and Mike out," replied Nanny.

"Are you ready, Rescueteers?" said King Brian. He knelt down out of sight in Nanny's hat. He pressed the palms of his hands together under his chin and looked up to the heavens.

"We're ready, King Brian," answered Nanny and Ned together as they tightened the stampede cords on their hats.

Nanny and Ned walked up to the skeleguard. Nanny had her skull trophy under her arm.

"Eh, excuse me, Sir!" Nanny said nervously.

"What are you two doing up here?" snarled the skeleguard.

"We came up to tell you there are lizard livers in the slelekitchen for the skeleguards," answered Ned.

"Lizard livers?" the skeleguard said with surprise. "For the skeleguards? "But I can't leave my post. These skeletrustees will be taking off in fifteen minutes I'll go then."

"But there won't be any lizard livers left if you wait," said Nanny. "We can watch the skeletrustees for you."

"No, that's out of the question," said the skeleguard. "I have a job to do here."

Nanny and Ned nodded and turned to walk away.

"Wait a minute," said the skeleguard. "It will take only a few minutes to run down to the skelekitchen. I'd love to taste those lizard livers. All right then, I'll take you up on your offer. I'll be right back," said the skeleguard and he took off in a hurry, clattering his way along as he hurried down the dusty rickety stairway.

"Now's our chance," said King Brian as he looked over the top of Nanny's hat.

"Open those cages, hurry, we don't have a moment to spare."

Nanny and Ned ran to the cages.

"Fran O'Toole and Mike Donovan," Ned said, as they approached the cages. "We're getting you out of here."

Fran and Mike froze. They were looking at two skelechefs with tall cowboy chefs hats, and one of them had his skull under his arm.

"This is it, Fran!" said Mike. "Our moment has come."

"You were a great friend to me all these years, Mike. I'll never forget you," Fran said, as he extended his hand out to Mike through the rails of his cage.

93

"We had some rare times didn't we Fran?" Mike said sadly while shaking Fran's hand.

"We sure did, Mike, we had the very best of times," Fran replied

"Fran, it's me!" said Nanny. "Nanny Reilly!

"And me!" said Ned. "Ned Franey!"

"Don't forget me," said King Brian laughing as he jumped up and over Nanny Reilly's chef's hat and landed on Fran's cage. Both Nanny and Ned took their hats off.

Fran O'Toole and Mike Donovan fainted, falling like dead people in a place that welcomed the likes.

"Wake up, wake up!" shouted Nanny. "The skeleguard will be back in a minute" Nanny patted Mike's cheeks. Mike was out for the count. "This is for human kind," said Nanny as she closed her eyes tight,

"May Fran and Mike
Wake up fast,
Before the skeleguard
Comes back."

She snapped her fingers and Fran and Mike woke up.

"What are you two doing here?" asked Fran in shock. "How did you get here? Looking at King Brian he asked, "Are you a leprechaun?"

"Never mind all that now," interrupted Mike Donovan. "We asked for a miracle, and we got one. Let's get out of here as fast as we can."

Nanny and Ned opened the cage doors and let Fran and Mike out. Then they heard skeleguards coming up the spiral stairway in a hurry.

"It's the skeleguards!" said Ned.

"I knew it was too good to be true," said Fran O'Toole. "We're doomed!"

Four skeleguards came through the door. "Leftover lizard livers," snarled one of them. "You're about to be leftover bones!" The skeleguards started to run towards the group.

At that very moment, Henry Daly landed on the rooftop with Bertie and Frosty and their reins in his mouth.

"It's Henry Daly!" yelled Ned.

"He's a sight for sore eyes," said King Brian.

"C'mon, hurry! Hurry!" shouted Henry Daly.

Nanny and Ned quickly put their hats back on and tied their stampede cords tight. Nanny and Fran O'Toole jumped on Frosty's back, Ned and Mike Donovan jumped on Bertie's back and King Brian jumped on Henry Daly's back. The skeleguards ran towards them. Henry Daly growled at the skeleguards. The hair stood up on his back and drool spilled from his mouth.

"You're about to be left over bones!" he growled as he took a step toward the skeleguards with King Brian on his back. The skeleguards stopped dead in their tracks! They weren't going to challenge that ferocious dog before them. None of them wanted to be left over bones!

"Fly away now, lads!" yelled King Brian

"Up up, and away, Frosty!" yelled Nanny.

"Up up, and away, Bertie!" yelled Ned.

"Up up, and away, Henry Daly!" yelled King Brian.

Bertie, Frosty, and Henry Daly jumped off the castle roof and flew away. They flew over Dreary Castle and the skelestation. Then they flew over the grounds of The Banshee's Cradle and the gates. They flew over the forest and landed back at Raven's Point.

Fran O'Toole and Mike Donovan were so happy. They jumped off the backs of Bertie and Frosty knelt on the ground and kissed it. They picked up several fistfuls of sand and tossed it in the air. They began laughing and hugging each other. Fran O'Toole did a cartwheel and Mike Donovan made a brave attempt at one. The Rescueteers laughed with them. Fran and Mike grabbed Nanny and Ned and hoisted them up on their shoulders and danced several steps of a jig. Then they all fell in the sand laughing.

"Sweet Mother," said Fran O'Toole. "We're alive and kicking."

"Thanks to King Brian's leprechaun magic, Nanny Reilly, Ned Franey and their talking dog, Henry Daly," said Mike Donovan patting Nanny and Ned on the back and Henry Daly on the head.

"It's time for us to go," said Fran. "I can't thank you all enough. How in the world did two children like yourselves become so brave?

"We were brave because we were on a mission for the good of human kind," answered Nanny.

"And animal kind," added Ned. Ned looked at Henry, and Henry Daly smiled back at Ned.

"That's two of the finest reasons to be brave," said Mike Donovan, "we'll never forget what you have done for us. If ever any of you need our help for any reason, our doors are always open to you.

"King Brian," said Fran, "If I ran into you under normal circumstances on any other day, I would ask you for three wishes. But today, I have a million wishes in one. Just standing here on the golden sand at Ravens Point. Thank you so much."

King Brian smiled at Fran and held the lapels of his waistcoat and said, "On a normal day, under normal circumstances Fran O'Toole, you wouldn't run into me."

Fran and Mike laughed and said their farewells; they knew this was very true what King Brian had just said. The only way someone would come across King Brian, was if he wanted them to. He's way to crafty to let just anyone run into him.

"I think it's time for me to say good day to you all," said King Brian, but before I go I think the two bravest children in Ireland ought to have a couple of nice blackthorn sticks." He snapped his fingers and two fine shillelaghs appeared in Nanny and Ned's hand. King Brian then reached for his own shillelagh and waved it at Nanny, Ned and Henry Daly and said the words,

"May the leprechauns be near you,
To spread luck along your way,
And may all the Irish angels
Smile on you today."

Nanny, Ned and Henry Daly said goodbye to King Brian, and then he disappeared.

"Holy moley," said Henry Daly, looking down at himself. "I'm still a black skeleguards dog! And you're still skelecooks. I wish we were our old selves again."

"Done," laughed King Brian's voice from afar, and sure enough, Henry Daly was a brindle dog again. Nanny and Ned's skeliforms disappeared and they too were back to there old selves wearing their cowboy hats and sitting on their ponies.

Nanny and Ned rode Bertie and Frosty back home along the beach with Henry Daly by their side. It was almost dawn. They were both very tired and very quiet. The sudden realization of their rescue mission hit them like a ton of bricks. What would have happened to them if the Banshee knew who they were?

"I don't want to go back into the Banshee's Cradle ever again Nanny," said Ned.

"Me either Ned," replied Nanny. "I'm glad it's all behind us, we won't ever have to worry about the Banshee staring us in the face again."

Little did Nanny, Ned and Henry Daly know what the future had in store for them. They now have, magical powers and ponies at their disposal for the good of human kind and animal kind. They have been called to rise. They are now, The Rescueteers!

THE END